CURSED BY FIRE

BLOOD & MAGIC: FIREBORN - ONE

DANIELLE ANNETT

> "Danielle Annett's BRANDED BY FIRE is scorching hot."
> —*Amazon Reviewer*

> "Branded by Fire is the best one yet (and the other 3 books in the series rock!)"
> —*Sapphyria's Book Blog*

Consumed by Fire

> "Aria is badass"
> —*Amazon Reviewer*

> "Another fast paced installment of the Blood & Magic series. Aria's sass and badassery keeps me coming back for more."
> —*Amazon Reviewer*

> "When an author can leave you hanging and wanting more; then that is a brilliant author."
> —*The Avid Reader*

Forged by Fire

> "Love it. Worth the wait"
> —*Amazon Reviewer*

> "The conclusion to this series was everything I expected and more. Besides thinking as aria as my bff and watching her grow thru the series I've also watched this author grow. I look forward to reading her next series! She surprised me in this last book and I'm so crazy that I rarely get surprised! "
> —*Amazon Reviewer*

For my daughter, Savanah.

Without you, I would have finished this book much sooner but perhaps this will teach you to always persevere.

And for Joshua. You will likely never read this but know that I love you.

Chapter One

Blood soaked my hands and coated the walls. It stained the concrete flooring of the abandoned warehouse and dripped from fixtures that hung from the ceiling, trickling like a slow rain.

My vision blurred and a wave of anguish rolled through me.

Dammit.

It wasn't fair.

My knees buckled. I slammed my fist down on the concrete floor, unable to register the pain. *How could I have let this happen?*

I stared down at the lifeless body of a child. A boy.

Kneeling in a pool of congealed blood, I reached out and ran my fingers through his chestnut hair. I ignored the now-cool moisture seeping into the denim of my pants and hugged his limp body to my chest. Rocking back and forth with him in my arms, I whispered apologies and murmurs of comfort. Not that he could hear me.

My chest constricted.

I was too late.

I hated myself for that.

His face was unrecognizable. Gone was the boy with the dimpled cheek and brilliant blue eyes. Left behind was a brutalized mass of flesh and bone—a ruined body drained of life at such a young age.

God, what had they done to him? I blinked several times to clear my vision.

His skin was mottled. Through a veil of blood, shades of blue and purple covered every inch of exposed skin. His clothes were torn. His right arm bent at an unnatural angle.

No child should have to go through this. I hugged him tighter to my chest and prayed he'd been dead before whoever had done this wreaked havoc on his body. Prayed that the twin punctures on his neck were the cause of death and that the rest had been—

Reality snapped like an elastic band, bringing me back to the present. I sat at my desk in Sanborn Place, ripped from the haunted memories of finding Daniel's broken body.

My fingers curled around his photograph, and I had to blink back the tears that threatened to fall.

It wasn't fair, and I didn't need anyone to tell me that life wasn't fair. I knew that already. It didn't mean I had to be okay with it.

I stared down at the wallet-sized photo now crumpled in my hands. He'd had a crown of chestnut hair, bright blue eyes, and a single dimple on his left cheek. It was the face of an innocent seven-year-old boy, cut down like he was little more than a calf brought to slaughter.

I struggled to link the image of this smiling boy to that of the ruined body I'd found less than forty-eight hours ago. My blood heated, and a turbulent rage rolled through me. One I had to fight to contain.

Breathe, Aria. Just Breathe.

A small flame licked my fingertips and singed the edge of the photograph. I sucked in a harsh breath and called back my fire.

Shit.

"Aria, you've got to stop staring at the kid. He's gone. Let it go."

My head jerked up at my boss's statement. I'd almost forgotten Mike was there.

He leaned back in his chair, his eyes scanning the never-ending stacks of paper that littered the surface of his desk. He hadn't even bothered to look up.

I shoved the photo into my desk drawer and slammed it hard enough that the sound echoed through the still room.

Mike lifted his gaze and cringed at the sight of my expression.

I wouldn't be surprised if my eyes had taken on an amber glow. That happened when I was upset and my fire simmered just beneath the surface. A hazard of being a pyrokinetic. Under normal circumstances, I would keep a lid on it. But these were not normal circumstances and I was more than *a little* upset right now.

"He was seven years old, Mike," I bit out through clenched teeth. "Seven!"

I shook my head and ran my fingers through the tangled strands of my waist-length brown hair.

The poor kid had barely lived.

Ever since the Awakening six years ago, when all things that went bump in the night had come out of the woodwork to play, safety had been tenuous at best. Vampires, shifters, mages, witches, and many more creatures from our nightmares had popped out of nowhere, having decided they were ready to integrate themselves into every day—or night—society. Kids like this, like seven-year-old Daniel Blackmore, were paying the price.

It'd been a shock to the human population to realize they weren't at the top of the food chain anymore. Six years later, we were all still adjusting. Hell, I was a pyrokinetic and even I'd struggled with the realization we weren't alone.

Daniel was just one of several recent casualties, and I was sick of it. The bastard who'd done this had gone too far this time. Children were off limits in my book. No exceptions. Ever. We all had to draw a line in the sand at some point, and this was mine.

Since I'd found his mangled body—broken and discarded as if he were nothing more than a piece of trash—I was determined to find the bastard who had killed him, and make him pay.

Oh, and it would be long and painful. I had no mercy for child murderers.

"Ari, I know what you're thinking, and the answer is no." Mike folded his arms across his chest and tried to adopt a stern expression. Instead, all he managed to do was look constipated.

I bit back the laugh that almost spilled out.

Mike Sanborn was an older man in his early fifties with a streak of silver in his otherwise midnight colored hair. Dressed in black slacks and a grey button-up shirt, his mid-section strained against the buttons. They looked like they might pop off at any moment and take someone's eye out.

The wrinkles around his eyes would lead you to believe he smiled a lot, but I knew better. Those lines were from his ever-present frown.

Mike might be my boss, but if he thought I was letting this go, he would be in for one hell of a rude awakening. I didn't take orders from anyone. Not even him, and he was well aware of that fact.

"I wasn't asking for your permission." My fingers drummed along my desk, and I was careful to take deep measured breaths to keep a lid on my pyrokinetic abilities. It's never in your best interest to burn down your place of employment.

"I don't give a rat's ass if you were asking. I'm telling you, Ari, let it go. You can't help him anymore. All you'll end up doing is getting yourself hurt, or worse, killed for your trouble."

That was the problem with people who had lived through the Awakening. Their only concern was self-preservation. Nothing else mattered.

Well, screw that because this little boy… he mattered.

I'd scrubbed my hands after finding his broken body, but when I looked down at them I still saw the blood. I still saw his empty eyes, and the pained expression captured by his death. I couldn't let this one go.

I stood up from my desk and grabbed my keys and daggers. I sheathed the twin blades on either side of my waist, grabbed my leather jacket, and made a beeline for the door. I needed to do something. Sitting here and arguing would not get me any closer to finding Daniel's murderer.

My boots made stomping noises across the carpet, and Mike crossed the room to intercept me.

Blocking the door, he glowered down at me, trying to use his size to intimidate me. Too bad shit like that didn't work. I was far from cowed.

"Move." My fingers twitched at my sides, and I fought the instinct to shove him out of my way. Mike was the closest thing to a father figure I had, and some lines, you just didn't cross. No matter how unreasonable the other party was being. Putting my hands on him was one of those lines.

"No." He shook his head and stubbornly pushed back his shoulders.

I ground my teeth together and waves of heat rolled off my back. Fire licked just beneath my skin. I scrubbed my hand over my face and cursed. He was being ridiculous. This entire situation was ridiculous.

"Mike, this isn't some game. A little boy died. He died! Does that even matter to you? I couldn't live with myself if I let this one go." I didn't bother to hide the accusation in my voice, and it only seemed to piss him off.

"What's your plan, Ari? You going to storm into the Coven and force them to tell you who murdered him? They won't tell you. They protect their own, and you're one person against an entire Coven of bloodthirsty vampires. Even the kid's parents know it's a lost cause. They've dropped the case and are focusing on burying their son. They're coming to terms with his death. And so should you. It's over."

We'd suspected that the culprit was a vampire. It was hard not to when Daniel's body had been riddled with bite marks. But, it wasn't over until I said it was over. I didn't care if I had to face the Coven alone. I had my own bag of tricks, and I was good at taking care of myself. Mike's known I was a pyrokinetic since the day he met me. This wasn't reason talking. This was him being overprotective, and I wasn't going to have it.

The Coven would know if they had a rogue in their territory. But if this was the work of one of their own, well then, I'd handle it. As well as the ramifications that would follow once I'd issued the bastard's sentence. We didn't have a court of law anymore. Vigilante justice was as good as it would get.

Jessica Blackmore had trusted me to find her little boy and bring him back. I'd failed. The least I could do was give her the head of the person responsible for killing him.

I smiled. I'd bring that back to her on a silver fucking platter.

Feeling the temperature in the room climb higher, I forced myself to slow my breaths on each inhale and exhale, trying to calm down and keep my pyrokinesis locked up tight. It wouldn't help the situation to start a fire. All it would do is prove to Mike that I wasn't in control, and I was in no mood for a lecture.

"Look, Ari, you're a merc. You take on a job when you have a client. There is no client so there is no job. We're not the police. We don't try to clean up the streets or bag the bad guys. We're mercenaries."

I snorted. Police. What a joke. We hadn't had a real police force in years. Not one that did a lick of good, anyway. We had the HPED, but they only handled human concerns and as soon as there was even a whiff of paranormal, they bailed. The boogeyman—as they'd put it—was above their pay grade.

I couldn't blame Mike for his way of thinking. Hell, two weeks ago I would have said the same thing. But this was different. Daniel was just a kid. I couldn't believe everyone was so willing to overlook a child's murder. People died, I got that, but I couldn't leave a murderer on the streets that didn't see the difference between right and wrong when it came to kids.

Lines. We all have them.

"Why don't—"

Mid-sentence I heard the distinct buzz of a cell phone. Mike dug his phone out of his left breast pocket and answered it without bothering to look at the screen.

"Sanborn," he said. Mike's face scrunched in confusion, a furrow forming between his brows. He listened for several moments, and I strained to hear the speaker's voice. "I don't—" He was cut off. "Well, it's just that—" Mike's scowl deepened, and his face grew flushed. "Fine."

With an angry curse, he hung up the phone and stared me down. Lifting my chin, I gave him my best "try me" stare. The one I knew drove him crazy.

"Looks like you're getting exactly what you asked for," he snapped.

"And what exactly is that?"

"That was Declan Valkenaar on the phone."

My eyes widened. Holy shit. The Pack Alpha? What the hell was he doing calling Mike?

"Turns out the dead kid is a shifter. His dad's not so willing to let his death go unanswered. You've got yourself a client. The Pacific Northwest Pack."

I raised an eyebrow and waited for the punch line. The Pack didn't outsource work. It didn't make any sense for them to hire me when they could handle the situation on their own and likely preferred to. None of the factions played well together, and shifters tended to look down on anyone who wasn't one.

He sighed in irritation but went on anyway. "Look, you searched for the boy for two weeks straight. You may not have found the kid in time, but you have more information than they do. They don't want to waste time starting from scratch. Unless you'd be willing to hand over your information and records?" Mike's voice had just a hint of hope to it.

I snorted. Fat chance of that.

He sighed. "That's what I thought. Your fee's been paid through an electronic transfer. In full."

This was out of left field. It made sense to hire me since I was already familiar with the case, but I felt like I was missing something. My thoughts must have shown because Mike added one more bit of detail.

"Also, since we're all under the assumption that the culprit is a vampire, the Pack is hoping to avoid any issues with the Coven. So, you're supposed to prevent a war." He grinned like it was funny. "Have fun."

I clenched my eyes shut and counted to ten. Awesome. Now it made perfect sense. The Pack and the Coven were always at one another's throats. There was no way the Coven would let anyone from the Pack come in and question them. I was being hired to play the middleman. This would suck.

Mike was right though. I was getting what I wanted. The gig paid well. Hiring a mercenary wasn't cheap, and Sanborn Place had a solid reputation, so we were priced higher than most. Not that I had contributed much to that reputation.

I was average. I got by with bravado and luck and little skill. My father taught me to fight when I was a teenager. He wanted me to be able to defend myself. But punching a bag with my papa wasn't the same as getting into a brawl with a vampire ten times stronger and faster than me or going head to head with a shifter who could rip my throat out in the blink of an eye.

I was strong in my own right, but my grasp on my pyrokinetic abilities wasn't great. Most paranormals were genetically stronger than me, yet somehow I still made my clients happy and kept myself alive.

Nico and Taylor were the veteran mercs who'd been the major contributors in recent years, but both were taking a hiatus after completing a gig that had pushed them to their limits.

Perfect fucking timing.

I sighed.

I would have done the job for free, but a paying gig meant Mike had no legitimate reason to stop me from taking it on. He had to earn a living too, and now that he worked behind a desk, he relied on the ten percent cut he got from me and the other mercs that passed through our doors.

The fee being paid in full and up front also meant I couldn't gripe about being wedged between two factions of paranormals. The relationship between shifters and vampires was notoriously volatile. I had a feeling that no matter how hard I tried to conduct a peaceful investigation, blood would spill. I just hoped it wouldn't be mine.

I was glad someone was willing to take a stand, but this wasn't adding up.

"Mike, we met the parents already and neither one of them is a shifter. I can see a shifter a mile away." Shifters had a way of moving, a predatory grace. Neither Patrick nor Jessica Blackmore had that.

Mike ran his fingers through his hair, giving his head a slight shake. "According to Declan, the kid's mom remarried when Daniel was four years old. Patrick Blackmore is his stepfather. Daniel had no contact with his biological father after the split."

If that was the case why did this guy care now? He hadn't seen his kid in three years, and all of a sudden he cared about him? Just as I was about to voice the question, Mike raised his hand to stop me.

"Before those gears in your head start turning, you should know that you won't be working this one alone."

I stared at him for half a beat. Did he seriously think he was up for this? I mean, he was great and all, but he'd been playing desk duty since the day he hired me. And in those two years, Mike had grown soft in the most literal way. A good twenty pounds of softness if you asked me. He was nowhere near the shape he needed to be in to hunt down murderous vampires. At best, he'd slow me down. At worst, he'd get us both killed.

Mike was a liability, and he knew it.

"Mike, there is no way you can partner with me. Don't be stupid. What would Marian say?" I hoped bringing his wife into it would knock some sense into him.

Mike glowered at me. "Well, thanks for the vote of confidence, brat. I wasn't talking about me, so don't bring my wife into this. Besides, if I wanted to be on this case, I would damn well be on it. But since this is an official Pack problem, you're going to have a Pack partner. Play nice." His feathers officially ruffled, Mike puffed out his chest and lumbered back to his desk, grumbling under his breath about smart-ass women and no damn sense.

I fought back an eye roll and smiled. I was sure I'd gotten under his skin when I'd brought up Marian, but she and I were on the same page when it came to Mike working in the field.

Marian kept nagging him to retire, said the job was too dangerous and was better suited for people my age. Frankly, I agreed. The fact that Mike was no longer active in the field did little to assuage her concerns when he routinely insisted on tagging along, claiming that it was strictly for observational purposes.

Observational my ass. I knew he missed the thrill of the chase. But he needed to come to terms with the fact that retirement was just around the corner.

I was going to miss seeing him every day when he finally hung up his hat for good. Mike had only been in my life for two years, but he was my rock. Filling the hole left by losing my parents at the age of seventeen.

I leaned on him more than I cared to admit. I'd never tell him that, though. No sense inflating his ego.

My need to rush out and bring vicious justice abated, I returned to my desk to skim through all of my files on Daniel's case.

I wasn't thrilled about working with a partner. I hadn't survived living alone on the streets for four years by trusting, or working well, with other people. And I wasn't about to start now. A partner required a certain level of trust that I just wasn't willing to put in just anyone.

Mike Sanborn and James Shields—my werewolf best friend — were the exceptions. Mike found me two years ago, slumming on the streets, taking on mercenary gigs that were basically suicide missions. After all, there weren't many options for a girl my age with no experience and no desire to expose her abilities. But my pyrokinetic powers gave me an advantage. Not that I made them public knowledge. Most would assume I was a witch, and I happily let people continue believing it. It was safer that way.

I'd come across James Shields in a shifter bar when I'd tried to let off some steam and gone a bit overboard. One too many drinks and grabby hands from a grizzly had set me on a warpath. Thanks to the one too many tequila shots, it didn't register that I was grossly outmatched, and I dove in swinging.

James stepped in and helped me mop the floor with the grizzly's head. For reasons I still don't know. But since then, he'd saved my ass more times than I could count. We'd only known one another for six months, but I trusted him to watch my back. Even if he was a wolf.

I knew when push came to shove that Pack always came first, but we hadn't crossed that bridge yet, and as far as I knew, he'd kept my secret.

I hadn't intended to tell him about me, and there'd been alcohol involved when I did. He'd taken the revelation in stride, and we'd been friends ever since.

Maybe I'd get lucky and the Pack would send him. Mike had used him before when he required shifter backup, and James never minded tagging along and earning a little extra money. It was doubtful since he wasn't an Alpha, but a girl could hope. Unlike most male mercs, he never bristled if I took the lead.

I'd worried in the beginning that he would spill my secret. Being a pyrokinetic made me a prime target for anyone wanting to exploit me to their advantage or eliminate a potential threat. As soon as my abilities manifested, my papa drilled into me the need to keep them a secret. Back then paranormals weren't public knowledge, and the fear was that I'd end up as some government lab rat.

Papa knew about psykers like myself, human beings born with psychokinetic powers. His grandfather had been one, though according to my Papa, he'd been an aerokinetic. Able to manipulate air and its currents.

I'd been lucky that he'd had some knowledge of the matter. He knew enough to teach me some basic meditation techniques, help me work on control, and teach me who I needed to avoid. Specifically, other psykers.

When I hit eighteen, my abilities grew stronger. Mike had later speculated that it had something to do with maturing and getting older. Regardless, I had a slip in control and burnt down my first apartment building. By accident, of course.

I'd been stressed out, overworked, and barely getting by. My fuse was short back then, and I had one hell of a nosey neighbor that knew just how to get under my skin.

But that slip-up had left me exposed.

Less than two hours later, a man had arrived at my burnt doorstep as I dug through the rubble of my meager belongings—

trying to salvage what I could—with an offer he thought I couldn't refuse.

I'd asked for a day to consider it, knowing there was no way in hell I'd accept. He'd promised to come back in the morning. As soon as he'd left, I'd packed what hadn't been ruined in the fire and hit the road.

He tried tracking me. It took three weeks to lose him and a year to stop looking over my shoulder. No one searches for someone they have no connections to that hard with good intentions.

To stay hidden, I kept to the streets. Being homeless had surprising perks. I had knowledge and contacts that otherwise I'd never have, and I developed reliable instincts and better fighting skills from having to defend myself on a regular basis.

See, the glass was always half full.

"So when does my partner arrive?" I rifled through my desk in search of my notebook. It wasn't much to look at. Just a worn leather cover with several hundred pages of what I deemed to be important information. One such piece of information was a growing list of Pack members and their roles. The shifters were a secretive bunch. I knew who some Pack Alphas and Betas were, but not all of them.

It was highly probable they'd send me one of the Clan Betas. Someone with enough authority to make decisions for the Pack and take out any potential threats. If that were the case, I would need to make sure I didn't expose myself. Easier said than done, but I didn't want to find myself on the Pacific Northwest Pack's most wanted list.

"No idea. But, Ari, I've got a bad feeling about this one. You wanted the kid to get justice, and he'll get it. You know how shifters are. They won't stop until they find the culprit. Why don't you just stay out of it and let them handle this their way?"

No way I would stand on the sidelines while the Pack took

over. Not happening. This was my case. I'd already poured blood and sweat into it.

I allowed my displeasure to wash over my face.

"Ari, don't give me that look. You know I'm only looking out for you. What would happen if the Pack found out you were a pyrokinetic?"

We'd had this conversation before. I didn't need to worry about that because it wouldn't happen.

If the Pack or Coven, or hell, even the witches discovered what I was, one of three things would happen. They'd either kill me because I was too big of a threat to leave living or they'd somehow find a way to control me and make me their little fire slave. If I had a heads-up early enough, I'd go for option three and run. Again.

I didn't want to leave. I'd put down roots here. But I'd die before I ever let someone else control me.

"Mike, you and I both know that won't happen. I'll be careful like I always am. Why don't you just tell me what fur ball they're going to saddle me with?" I smiled when I found my notebook in my desk's bottom drawer. "Finally." I pulled the notebook out and leaned over it as I scanned the coffee stained pages within for likely candidates. It was doubtful the Pack would send a Clan Alpha. They were too important to spare for sleuthing.

Packs were made up of Clans, smaller groups of shifters with their own Alphas and Betas who reported to the Pack leadership. There were six Clans within the Pacific Northwest Pack I knew of. Each was led by a single—or joint if mated—Clan Alpha, and all served under Declan Valkenaar, the Pack Alpha.

The Pacific Northwest Pack encompassed Clans Wolf, Cat, Feloidea, Muridea, Canidae, and Big, which encompassed, well, anything really big. Bears, a handful of water buffalos, and if memory served, a rhinoceros shifter or two.

Mike noisily cleared his throat. "Uh, hey, Ari…"

"God, I hope whoever they send isn't a complete moron. If

I'm going to be stuck with a Pack partner, the least they can do is give me someone competent."

Mike noisily cleared his throat again.

"What?" I looked up from my desk and scowled at the tall man standing just inside the office, casually leaning against the doorframe. He had tousled brown hair and steely grey eyes. High cheekbones and a strong jaw formed his face and a hint of stubble dusted his jawline. It was not enough to appear unkempt, but just enough to give a roguish impression. Dressed in black jeans, a black tee, and a black leather jacket, he oozed tall, dark, and handsome with deadly intent.

I shoved my notebook into the top drawer of my desk. Shit.

"That would be this furball right here," James said, an arrogant grin lifting the corner of his mouth.

I let my head fall to the surface of my desk, then for good measure, I none too gently knocked my forehead on its smooth surface, one, two, three times. Dammit, I couldn't believe I'd just called him a freaking furball!

My cheeks warmed, and heat crept up my neck.

On the upside, at least my partner was someone I actually knew and trusted to watch my back.

"You all done with the show?" he asked.

I lifted my head and glared at him, then dropped my head to the desktop once more before sitting up and rubbing the sting away. "Yeah, I'm done." This wasn't going to be as bad as I'd expected. James Shields was a wolf and having him as my partner was going to make this gig a lot more tolerable than I'd expected. "So you're my partner?"

James nodded. "Yeah, I'm your partner." He sauntered into the room, his eyes scanning the articles pinned to the exposed brick walls. "Think you can play nice for once?"

"Hey!" I admonished. "I'm always nice to you."

He snorted and wandered further into the room, moving with a confident and carefree grace, his gaze now locked on mine.

If he weren't the closest thing I had to a best friend, I'd be drooling like the rest of society when he walked into a room.

"Sure, you are. You ready to get reckless?" His lips curved to one side, and his eyes pulled me out of my seat.

I smiled. He knew me all too well. "Absolutely."

I grabbed my messenger bag and followed James out of the office, aware of Mike's disapproving gaze following my every step.

Chapter Two

J ames led the way to the attached basement parking garage, and my mouth watered at the sight of his 1970 Boss 302 Mustang.

Damn. That car was every man's wet dream. Mine too, if I were being honest. The Mustang sported a custom black on black paint job with black rims, blacked-out taillights, and black leather interior.

It had badass written all over it.

"So when are you going to let me take her for a spin?" I asked, feigning indifference. I really wanted to drive it, but James was such a control freak when it came to his *pride and joy.*

James laughed, his smooth timbre echoing through the vacant lot. He shook his head, his tousled, dark brown hair almost hiding the mischievous glint in his eyes. "Never, Ari. Never."

He opened the driver side door and leaned his elbow against the roof with a wicked grin on his face as he looked me over with a wry grin.

I pushed out my bottom lip and gave him the closest thing to a doe-eyed expression I could conjure up.

"We've been on gigs before where I saved your life. You'd think that'd earn me at least a lap around the block." I folded my arms across my chest and arched a brow.

"I've saved your ass as many times as you've saved mine. We're even." James slid into the car in one fluid motion, not bothering to hear my response.

I rolled my eyes—I'd get my hands on his keys eventually—and opened the passenger side door, climbing in beside him.

"I'm a perfectly safe driver." My Honda Civic was still in one piece.

James put the Mustang into drive and navigated his way out of the garage. "Not happening." With his eyes on the road, I took in his strong jaw and sharp, angular nose. Heavy brows rested over steely grey eyes that evolved into liquid mercury when his wolf rose to the surface.

I pursed my lips together. "This isn't over," I warned.

"It never is," he said with a wolfish grin that had me instinctively smiling back.

I caught myself and schooled my expression, but he'd already seen it.

James winked, and I fiddled with the knobs on the stereo in an attempt to hide the blush rising to my cheeks. He did that sometimes. Flirted. Why, I wasn't sure.

James was a friend. My *best friend.* I didn't see him as anything more, and I was almost certain he didn't see me as anything more either. But sometimes he'd give me a look. You know, the kind filled with all sorts of innuendo, and I'd get all flustered for no reason. Because obviously, I had to be imagining it. Right? Only sometimes, I wasn't entirely certain.

If you saw him, you'd have the same problem. The man oozed sex appeal.

Don't go there, I chided myself and sighed. Now really wasn't the time to contemplate the intricacies of male and female platonic relationships.

Setting those thoughts aside, I turned my mind back to the task at hand.

We were on our way to see Daniel Blackmore's biological father. James and I had never partnered up on anything involving the Pack, so Pack secrets weren't something we'd ever had to navigate. And with shapeshifters, *everything* was a secret.

They were one of the most private factions. Not that I could blame them. Humans feared shapeshifters, and humans tended to treat what they feared with thinly veiled hatred. Most saw them as animals on the verge of losing their marbles any moment.

I couldn't blame the shifters for their secrets. But, I sure as hell could try and pry as many of them as possible out of James.

I didn't know how forthcoming he would be. Partners or not, James would only share so much, and I had a feeling that it would be limited to only what he considered relevant to the case, so I'd start there.

"Who's the father?" Merc 101, it was always best to start with the obvious.

"Eric Delaney. He's a wolf. Lives on the South Hill."

Hmmm… Must be doing all right for himself since the divorce. The South Hill lay on the nicer side of Spokane, Washington. Houses were nestled close, but the views of the city were stunning. The cramped houses were a fair tradeoff for a lower crime rate and cleaner neighborhoods.

If I could afford a house on that side of town, I'd live there too.

"So, I take it the kid took his mom's last name? They don't match. And, not that I'm complaining, but why did Delaney ask for help? Why isn't he moving on like Jessica and her husband seem to be?"

James's broad shoulders lifted in a shrug. "I think the last name was agreed upon during the divorce." His knuckles tightened on the steering wheel, but his eyes stayed firmly in front of him. "Eric called our Alpha yesterday morning. I didn't hear the conversation, but no shapeshifter would let their child's murderer go unpunished. He may have been off the grid for the last few years, but Daniel was still his son. He was still Pack. Even if none of us knew it."

Whoa. That had to sting. "You didn't know Daniel was being raised in the human world?"

He shook his head. "We didn't even know it was possible for a non-shifter to bear a shapeshifter child. I don't think Eric did either. Probably why he let Jessica take the kid in the first place. He must have figured Daniel was strictly human and better off in the human world. The rest of us did. Most shifter children experience their first…" He trailed off. *Damn.*

"Experience their first what?"

The corner of his mouth lifted in a rueful grin. "It's not important to the case."

I rolled my eyes. "Fine. Who's his Alpha?"

I didn't know who Clan Wolf's Alpha was, or where their Clan house was located. But I knew Declan Valkenaar lived here in Spokane, WA, in the heart of the Pack lands. The rest of the Clan Alphas would live within the surrounding territories and most of their identities were kept private.

It was safer that way. No targets for the humans intent on destabilizing the shapeshifters.

James smiled again and trained his eyes in my direction. "Nice try."

I pouted. "Alpha names aren't secret. All of Washington knows it's Declan at the helm of the Pacific Northwest Pack."

James snorted. "True enough, but that doesn't mean we shout it from the rooftops, either. We like our privacy."

I rolled my eyes and moved on to my next question. I knew a losing battle when I saw one.

"Is it possible that Eric could be involved in his son's murder? That this is all just a front?" I didn't like the idea that a parent could harm their own child, but it had to be asked. If Delaney had been away from his son all these years, it made me wonder just how much his son meant to him.

James gave me a sideways look, his piercing gaze asking me if I was stupid.

"What?" I worried my lower lip. It was a legitimate question.

"No shifter would harm a child. Let alone one of their own flesh and blood."

I fought the urge to roll my eyes. "You just said he'd been off the grid. He all but abandoned his son which I'm pretty sure is something no shifter would do either. Can we really afford to make any assumptions here?"

A snarl worked its way up James's throat. "You ask an awful lot of questions."

"That is part of the job." I drummed my fingers along the window's edge. "Why is the Pack helping him? Eric Delaney left, and as far as either of us are aware, his shifter son had been living in the human world separate from the Pack."

I got the same sideways look.

Fine, yeah whatever, stupid question. "Do you know the situation between Eric Delaney and Jessica Blackmore?" When Daniel had first gone missing, Jessica and her husband had assumed he'd been taken for ransom. They were well off and lived in a safe neighborhood with little paranormal activity. If there was bad blood between Jessica and Eric, it was possible it had started out as a simple abduction. Maybe he wanted to use Daniel as leverage against his ex-wife and something went wrong?

"Not much. Only that they separated three years ago, and that during the divorce he asked for leave. The Pack didn't get involved since no one had expected the relationship to last in the first place."

"Why wouldn't you expect it to last?"

"Relationships between shifters and non-shifters are rare. Those of us around when Eric courted Jessica saw it going downhill fast."

I mulled that over in my mind as we made our way up Freya Street. "How does that work exactly? I assumed shifters weren't allowed to marry non-shifters?"

James gave me a curious glance, probably reading more into my question than I'd intended. "Any Pack member can marry outside the Pack. It's not frowned upon per se. But non-shifters are prohibited from living inside the Compound. We don't trust outsiders. It can make a relationship… difficult."

"Hey!" I smacked his arm. "I can be trusted."

"You're an exception," he said.

Liar. I bit my tongue and waited for him to continue.

"It would be difficult to maintain a relationship when the core of who we are lives within the Pack. Not impossible," he added. "Just… difficult."

We pulled up to a single-story home. James killed the engine, and we both stepped out of the car. The house matched the modern style of the neighborhood, but where the other homes on the block were pristine with manicured lawns, Eric Delaney's house was a wreck—peeling paint, overgrown shrubbery, debris piled on the side of the house.

Making sure my blades were visible within my leather jacket, I left my bag behind and made my way up the short pathway leading from the street to the front door. James stalked behind me. He gave the impression he was the muscle in this situation, which he was.

James didn't need the money a gig provided. He owned Hills Fitness, and between that and his work with the Pack, he was doing just fine. But he never passed on a case involving vamps. In fact, he usually went out of his way to insert himself into them now that I thought about it.

Things were hostile between the Pack and the Coven so I'm sure the information he gleamed was useful. I didn't mind. I owed no loyalties beyond those to my clients. Though I'm sure if the Coven knew about it, they certainly would mind. But hey, what they didn't know wouldn't hurt them.

We had a routine already, and he hung back and let me do the talking. Most people were intimidated enough by his presence. He didn't have to work all that hard at it.

Climbing the few steps to the door, I rapped three times and waited for a response.

No one answered.

I knocked three more times and again waited, doing my best not to fidget. Patience was not a virtue of mine.

After several long moments, there was the distinct sound of a lock retracting and the door opened just a crack.

"What do you want?" the man behind the door asked in a gruff voice.

I could make out his olive skin tone and fall of chestnut hair, just like Daniel's. "Eric Delaney?" I asked.

"Who's asking?" The words were slurred.

"I'm Aria Naveed. I'd like to speak with you about your son's death."

"You mean my son's murder?" he growled. His eyes took on an eerie shifter glow, and I had to fight my instincts to take a step back.

"Yes, his murder," I said, in what I hoped was a calm and soothing voice. Judging by the metallic sheen to his eyes, his wolf was riding close to the surface. "I'd like a few moments of your time to interview you and see if you might be able to present any leads. I'm trying to bring down your son's killer, and I could use your help to do that."

Eric Delaney looked crazed. His eyes glowed, but they were also clearly bloodshot, and his hair was a mess. Sticking out on all sides it looked like he hadn't used a hairbrush in ages and couldn't be bothered with a finger-comb either.

I wondered if maybe he was having trouble sleeping, then mentally slapped myself as soon as the thought crossed my mind.

Of course he was having trouble sleeping. His kid was just murdered.

Unless he'd willingly caused his son's murder, he wouldn't be getting any sleep any time soon.

Eric peered over my shoulder and eyed James up and down before his eyes strayed to the car parked at the curb. His nostrils flared as he inhaled our scent, and I watched recognition flash.

All color drained from his face, and he began alternately eyeing the car at the curb and James. Why did he keep staring at the car? It was probably one of the most beautiful vehicles on the streets of Spokane, but I wasn't sensing admiration in Eric's eyes. I was sensing fear.

Why would he be afraid of someone in his own Pack? His own Clan for that matter? Both Eric and James came from Clan Wolf.

I didn't know what James did for the Pack, but whatever it was, it was scaring the hell out of Delaney.

Taking a step back, Delaney opened the door wider and motioned for us to come in.

I moved to take a step into the house, but before I could pass the threshold, James slid in past me, blocking my way. He stood still as a statue for a tense moment before making his way farther into the house. Stupid shifter habits, always thinking women needed to be protected. James knew better than most that I was capable of looking out for myself.

Rolling my eyes, I followed James into the house and was hit with the overwhelming stench of booze and sweat. I wrinkled my nose and did my best to breathe through my mouth as Eric led us through the entryway and into the living area.

James and I sat down on the beat up leather sofa and waited for Delaney to settle himself in the matching chair directly across from us. He avoided eye contact, focusing instead on his trembling hands balanced on his knees.

The smell in the room was all encompassing. I could only

imagine how it affected James with his enhanced shifter senses. I had to blink my eyes just to keep them from watering, but I was fighting a losing battle.

Taking a deep breath, and then instantly regretting it, I composed myself the best I could and tried to size up Eric Delaney. He was small for a man. Around my height of five-foot-seven and much thinner than I would have expected for a shifter. Most shifters were built with corded muscles and an athletic body. Eric was so thin he appeared sickly almost like he was malnourished.

I surveyed the room and spotted several empty bottles strewn across the carpet and several shards of broken glass, likely remnants from previous bottles. There was a questionable pile in the carpet near the window, and the flies buzzing around it led me to believe it was vomit.

Gross.

I returned my gaze to Eric and took another breath through my nose. *Dammit.* You'd think I'd of learned my lesson after that first one. The stench hit my nostrils, and I inwardly gagged. God, what had he been doing, drinking himself into a coma?

"Mr. Delaney, when was the last time you saw your son?"

He didn't seem to hear me. He continued to wring his hands and look back and forth between James and me with a wide-eyed expression.

"Mr. Delaney?" I prompted again.

Still nothing. I pinned James with a questioning look.

He sighed. "Eric, I'm not here to hurt you. Answer her questions. Please."

I raised a brow, but James didn't bother answering my unspoken question.

"But you're the—"

James shook his head and sent a pointed look in my direction. Eric caught the meaning and closed his mouth before visibly swallowing.

What had Eric been planning to say? What was James hiding from me? I chewed my bottom lip. This whole Pack secrecy thing was going to get old. Fast.

"If you're not here to kill me, then why are you here?" His words were little more than a whisper.

Wait a minute. Did he just say kill? Holy hell! I was missing something because why the hell would anyone assume that my best friend was a murderer?

James sighed again. "I'm here to work with Miss Naveed. She isn't Pack, and this is Pack business. Just answer her questions truthfully."

Eric nodded, and though his shoulders seemed to relax, he still sent worried glances toward James every few seconds.

I repeated my question but couldn't help my gaze straying to James, who firmly ignored me. His eyes were glued to Delaney, and I could tell from the clench of his jaw that he was holding himself back from meeting my gaze with effort.

"Umm… the last time I saw Daniel was about three years ago," he answered.

I turned my attention back to Eric. James could be dealt with later. "And why is that?" I gentled my voice as to not spook the man.

"Err… I have a drinking problem," he whispered, a deep flush rising up his neck. "Jessica, my wife—" He scowled and shook his head. "Ex-wife I mean. After she left, she refused to let me see him."

"Is there anyone who may have wanted to use your son against you?"

"No."

"Are you sure? You don't have any enemies who—"

"No." Delaney was shaking his head. "Look, I don't go out. I don't have friends. I can't think of any reason someone would want to use my son to get to me."

"Did your wife have—"

Eric looked down between his feet and pulled at his hair with an agitated noise. "No. Jessica isn't the type of woman to make enemies. She's pleasant to everyone. She doesn't make waves. It isn't her style. She's demure. Submissive. She doesn't even gossip behind other women's backs."

"It's been years since you two—"

"I know my wife!" Delaney pushed away from the sofa and paced. Despite being in his human skin, he looked very much like the agitated wolf he was right now.

"Eric." James's voice was quiet but echoed with strength. Eric instantly stilled. "Did you have anything to do with Daniel's murder?"

"No."

"Do you believe your ex-wife capable of any involvement in his murder?"

"No."

"Do you believe her husband could—"

A growl rumbled deep in Eric's chest. "I don't know, but if he did…" He let the threat hang in the air.

Chapter Three

James and I spent close to an hour at Delaney's house, grilling him for any information he may have held relevant to Daniel's death.

We still came away with nothing. James's shifter senses let him know that Eric never lied, and while helpful in eliminating Eric from the pool of suspects, it still didn't give us anything to go on. No leads. No clues. Nothing.

I kicked a piece of trash on the porch as I headed towards James's Mustang. "I need something to go on. Anything. The smallest little crumb," I muttered under my breath.

James gave me a sideways glance, letting me know that he could hear me despite my efforts, but he didn't comment. Instead, he hung back by the door as I continued down the steps. I may have sounded like an annoyed teenager as I stomped my way to the car, but what did I care?

I climbed into the Mustang and stewed on my frustration until James opened the door.

I kept going back to the why. Why Daniel? Why him of all the kids out there? The vampire who attacked him had to have known he was a shifter. Their senses were enhanced enough to catch even a hint of shifter genes in a person, so why follow through?

From what I'd been told, vampires didn't like the taste of shifter blood. It didn't provide the same surge of energy. Daniel Blackmore was the first shifter/human child I'd heard of. Could he even shift? Did it matter?

I wondered if his blood would taste the same as a full-blooded shifter. Was there a chance that it would appeal even more to a vampire?

Daniel had been snatched on a quiet street away from the city. He lived in a low crime neighborhood with little paranormal presence. Regardless of his half-breed status, I didn't think this was a random case of wrong place, wrong time. No. Whoever took Daniel took him for a specific reason.

I just needed to figure out what it was.

James shifted the Mustang into drive and pulled away from the curb. He slid on his sunglasses and kept his eyes firmly in front of him. A clear indication that he wasn't interested in talking.

Sucked to be him.

"What did you say to Delaney?" I asked as we headed back into downtown Spokane.

James didn't say anything. Didn't even bother to look in my direction.

I drummed my fingers noisily on the passenger-side door.

"I told him the Pack would send him some help, and that we were putting him into a rehab program."

"Does he want that?"

James shrugged. "I doubt it, since he didn't check himself in the first time around, but it doesn't matter what he wants now. He needs to get sober. That's all there is to it."

I digested that tidbit of information. Guess the Pack did what they thought was best, and while I agreed Eric needed to get sober, that didn't mean it should be forced on him. There was a reason things like this needed to be voluntary. He should have a choice in the matter. If he didn't, I wasn't all that confident that sobriety would stick. You couldn't help people who didn't want to be helped.

My thoughts wandered back to his initial fear. Why was he afraid of James, and why did he assume James was there to kill him?

I tried to find the best way to phrase my next question. I didn't really expect James to tell me. The glasses alone were my cue to shut up. I just happened to be a bad listener.

"What do you do?" I asked him, my voice casual as I gazed out of the passenger-side window, keeping James in my peripheral.

He tilted his head in my direction. "You know what I do. I run the gym."

Sure, James owned Hills Fitness Center, but I knew as well as he did that he didn't actually work there daily. And the gym wouldn't explain Eric's fears.

"Not your day job. What do you do for the Pack?"

Each member played a part within the Pack's hierarchy, and while most still had a day job, their main occupation lay within the Pack. It could be as minor as working in the kitchens or as major as running Pack security or being a teacher for their young.

James remained silent. After several long minutes I wondered if he would answer me at all and was getting ready to ask him something else about the case when he heaved a sigh and pulled over to the side of the road. He ignored the angry honks that came from cars swerving to avoid him and killed the engine. He sat still for a moment before removing his glasses and turning to face me.

Oh dear, shit was about to get serious.

"I'm the Pack's Hunter," he said in a grim voice, staring me straight in the eyes. Mercury flecks dancing in his gaze.

Holy shit! He was the Hunter? I schooled my expression to

hide my shock. I'd been sleuthing around for an entire year without a hint of the Hunter's identity. This was big. Like five-hundred-pounds big. I couldn't believe he'd been right under my nose!

That meant—I froze and my eyes widened.

A muscle ticked in James's jaw but he waited out the silence.

"The bear from a year ago. That was you?"

James nodded.

Holy shit!

About a year ago, a bear shifter had gone rogue and killed an entire community. He'd killed over a hundred people and injured another three hundred in a fit of uncontrollable rage on the outskirts of Cheney, a small town about a half hour from Spokane.

It had taken Declan and a group of other shifters just under forty minutes to assemble and get to Cheney once word of the bear hit their ears. A lot could happen in that amount of time, and rumor was, not much was left when they'd arrived. It'd been the Hunter to bring him down.

No one knew who or what breed of shifter he was. But a Hunter was supposed to be the strongest shifter in a Pack. A shifter more dominant than any Alpha, and who stood outside the Pack hierarchy.

I stared wide-eyed at him for a few seconds while I tried to figure out what to say. I could see the worry and fear in his eyes. Did he think that being the Hunter would make me see him differently?

My silence must have indicated something, because before I could respond, he continued, "I'm the one responsible for delivering Pack justice." He angled away from me and his usual commanding tone was now edged with defeat.

"Are you not very good at it?" I knew James well enough to know that issuing justice wasn't really the problem. He may be the cold, calm, and collected type, but he was the best man for the job. I couldn't believe I'd never suspected him before.

"No, that's the problem. I'm good at what I do. Maybe too good."

No, the problem wasn't that he was good. It was the waste of a life. James didn't turn away from killing, but he didn't kill if he didn't have to. We'd had to kill in the line of duty before, but James only ever did it as a last resort. When a shifter turns rogue, they lose all sense of humanity. You can't come back from that, but you don't know what you're doing. You're not in control anymore. The beast is.

I gazed out the window, a pair of crows picked at a carcass of what I could only assume had been a deer based on the size of the body. I sniffed the air, the slightly cloying scent of decay coming through the AC vents. "How long have you been the Hunter?"

James shrugged. "I don't really remember a time when I wasn't."

I sucked in a breath. "You weren't expected—not when you— I mean, they wouldn't send in a child. Right?"

His silence was deafening.

My blood boiled. How dare they? No one could expect a child to be ready to kill. Let alone kill someone that they grew up with in the Pack. What if he'd had to kill a family member or a mentor? How could they?

Had James ever had to hunt down someone he loved? I shivered at the thought. James didn't need my anger right now though. He needed my acceptance. My understanding.

I could give him that.

I sighed, drawing his gaze again. "Do you need to talk about your feelings now?" I asked, my tone light and teasing.

"You're a real piece of work, you know that?" He lightly punched me in the shoulder.

"Sure do. It's a wonder you've put up with me as long as you have."

James smiled, a real smile that met his steely grey eyes. "You know, I think that all the time."

I punched him in the shoulder back. "Jerk."

James flashed his teeth in a feral grin as he pulled the car back into traffic.

"Hey, Ari."

"Yeah?"

"We good?"

I smiled. "Always."

Chapter Four

The rest of the day went by in a blur. After meeting with Eric, James and I called it a day, making plans to speak with Mrs. Blackmore and her husband the following morning. I knew James was itching to make headway in the case. I was just as eager for justice as he was, but we didn't have any leads.

I was exhausted, so when he made up an excuse about needing to take care of some Pack obligation, I didn't object.

We both knew he was lying. Whether for my benefit or his own, I wasn't sure. But Daniel was already gone. There wasn't anything that couldn't wait until tomorrow.

Two weeks of sleepless nights while I searched for Daniel, only to discover I was too late, had taken its toll. That, coupled with the stress of the hunt, put me on edge, and I could feel myself burning out.

I took the bone James offered and had him drop me off at my apartment. Mike would have my car dropped off later in the evening, and I didn't need to go anywhere else today.

It was only four in the afternoon, but my body didn't care. It craved sleep and food in no particular order. I dragged my exhausted self up the first flight of stairs on my way to my single-bedroom apartment on the fourth floor.

"Hey, Mel," I said hi to my neighbor perched on the metal railing near the top of the first set of stairs. Her ebony mane fell in waves down her back and blended into blue-black feathers that covered her bird-like wings.

"Hey, Aria," she said around a mouthful of food. She clutched a small basket in her arms, with a smile spread across her face like she'd just won a prize.

I couldn't help the grin that stole across my face. "Stealing from Ryan again?" I asked.

Melody's smile widened and she took another bite from her stash with an enthusiastic nod.

Ryan was a musician who lived in our building. And Melody seemed to have a thing for him. Being a Harpy, she expressed her attraction by stealing. A strange method, but it seemed to do the job because, like every time before, Ryan came storming down the stairs, the heavy footfall of his boots thundering with each step.

"Melody!" he shouted before he'd even come into view. "Where is it?"

I smiled as I continued on my way. You'd think he'd learn by now.

"What is your problem?" he shouted.

"If you weren't open to sharing, you shouldn't have left this out for me," Melody said innocently.

I snorted but kept my mouth shut as their words echoed through the stairwell.

"Left it out? Left it out! Putting my food and belongings inside of my locked apartment behind locked cabinets is not leaving it out!"

I snickered. Some humans, despite living beside paranormals, still didn't have a clue how they ticked. And Melody—she loved a challenge.

Ryan's yelling and Melody's ruse at innocence faded with each step. Their banter just like any other day. I envied them a little if I were being entirely honest with myself. Envied that they had someone to fight with. Someone to go toe to toe with. Despite how things might look, I knew Ryan wasn't immune to Melody's ways.

When I reached the third flight, my thighs had begun to burn. Stupid stairs. Stupid elevator. I eyed the sliding metal doors with disdain as I took a moment to catch my breath. I was getting soft and needed to switch from weight training to cardio.

Especially as I realized that a small part of me wanted to step inside the cold metal box and lean against the cool inside wall until it chimed on my floor, but I couldn't. I knew that a single step inside, without the doors even closing, would send me into a spiraling panic.

Stupid elevator. I was definitely going to need to increase my cardio workouts. I sighed and pushed on.

One flight to go.

I could faintly hear Melody screech that it was Ryan's fault that she'd stolen his food. That he never should have left it out for her to find if he didn't want to share. I'd helped him install the locks that now covered every cabinet and closet within his apartment, knowing they wouldn't keep her out. The added security only encouraged her. A good neighbor would have told him as much. I wasn't a good neighbor. And it was too much fun letting him figure it out on his own.

With my apartment door in sight, I dug through my messenger bag for my keys. The elevator pinged, and I jerked my head up to see who'd arrived on my floor. There were only three apartments on the fourth floor, and aside from mine, the others were vacant. At least, I thought they were.

I didn't recognize the man who stood inside though his head was bowed. His jet black hair hid most of his features, but the military-style boots weren't something your average Bob or Joe wore around town.

The hairs on the back of my neck rose.

He stepped out of the elevator, distracted with the phone in his hand before he looked up and his gaze collided with mine.

He froze.

Startling blue-grey eyes, so clear it was like looking into a pool of water, met mine with a flash of recognition. But that couldn't be right.

Sharp cheekbones and a square jaw enhanced his full mouth. I'd never seen him before, but I was starting to wish that maybe I had.

I dropped my keys and cursed before bending to retrieve them.

What the hell? I was never clumsy.

The man walked towards me, and I tried not to stare at him as he drew closer. He was as beautiful and deadly as the daggers I kept at my waist, and dammit if I didn't want him. Clearly, it'd been too long if I was even considering jumping the stranger beside me.

"Anything I can help with?" he asked, interrupting my thoughts.

He crouched beside me and the smell of rainstorms assailed my senses. I paused longer than normal before answering him.

"No. I'm good. Thanks." I stood to my full height, and he followed suit. I had to fight the urge to step back. He was way too close.

I moved to go around him, and he shifted his stance to let me pass.

"Are you visiting someone in the building?" I asked as I approached my door. I stood with keys in hand and waited for his response. He was good looking, I'd give him that. But the way he was looking at me had my hackles rising and I'd learned a long time ago to always trust my instincts.

He shook his head. "No. I just moved in."

"On the fourth floor?"

He nodded, his gaze curious as if he were waiting to see my reaction.

I kept my expression bland and did my best not to scowl. I liked my privacy. And I'd enjoyed having the fourth floor all to myself for the past year now. "Well, welcome to the neighborhood. It was nice meeting you…"

"Inarus. Inarus Ryholt."

"Inarus." I repeated the name, liking the way it sounded. "What is that? Libyan?"

"Egyptian," he corrected.

I was half Iranian, and I'd always had a fascination with Middle Eastern countries. Though Egypt was largely situated in North Africa, it was still considered a part of the Middle East.

I didn't think Inarus was strictly Egyptian. His complexion was a little too fair. But that explained the exotic lift to his eyes and the chiseled jawline.

"Hmmm." I didn't know what else to say after that, so I fumbled with my keys and gave him a wave.

God, I was an idiot. A wave? When he was two feet in front of me. I'd smack myself in the forehead if that wouldn't just make things worse.

I struggled to insert the right key into the deadbolt without further adding to my humiliation. I didn't even have that many keys on my key ring. I could feel his gaze on my back, which seriously was not helping.

Neither was the fact that he hadn't moved. Shouldn't he be going to his own apartment?

Inarus looked like the kind of man who cracked skulls for a living. I wasn't one to judge, being in my current line of business, but his proximity put me on edge. Instinctively, I called my fire close to the surface.

Good looks and a muscular body didn't earn you any trust points in my book.

"Seriously, what the…" I muttered aloud and then cursed when I realized I was putting my key in upside down.

Dammit. Today was not my day. Finally unlocking the mechanism, I pushed the door open. I looked back over my shoulder to see Inarus still standing in the same spot. Not creepy at all.

I gave him one last wary look before stepping into my apartment and quickly shutting the door. I threw the deadbolt, then locked the doorknob too, just in case, before checking the windows and making sure they were all locked.

You could never be too safe.

Once my quick assessment was complete, and I confirmed that my apartment was secure, I tossed my keys and messenger bag on the small dining room table and headed straight into my bedroom at the end of the narrow hallway.

My apartment was simple. I was a minimalist. It made it easier to relocate on short notice if I needed to and it kept the clutter to a minimum so I didn't have to clean all that often.

On the right was the living and dining area with a small open kitchen. I'd decorated my humble abode with a variety of flea market finds that included mismatched wood dining room chairs, a circular steel-topped table, and a navy blue sofa.

To the left down a narrow hallway was my bedroom and the single bathroom, sectioned off from the rest of the apartment. It wasn't anything fancy but it suited my needs, and the rent was dirt cheap compared to others in the area, so I couldn't complain.

Once in my room, I kicked off my military-style black leather boots and peeled off my jeans and leather jacket, exchanging them for a soft pair of grey yoga pants and an oversized hoodie that said cute but psycho. It was probably true.

I gave my boots a cursory glance.

When I was home, I preferred to be barefoot, but meeting Inarus in the hall made me question if I should slip them back on.

He hadn't done anything overtly threatening, but you never knew when you'd need to run for the hills or kick someone in the balls. And steel-toed boots did a hell of a lot more damage than bare feet did.

I looked down at my toes and wiggled them in the carpet. The purple polish on them did me no favors in the kick assery department.

"Don't make a big deal of this," I chided myself.

He was a neighbor. Neighbors were totally normal to have. For once I would try to refrain from being the paranoid nut who thought everyone was out to get her.

I padded on bare feet to my kitchen. My cupboards were sparse, stocked with only the essentials. My refrigerator was equally bare, but I had what I needed to make a sandwich. I wasn't home often, and when I was, it never seemed to make sense to cook for a party of one.

A lot of the time, Marian would send leftovers with Mike for me to take home. She was a godsend, because without her, it would have been years since I'd had a home cooked meal. I didn't do domestic. It was a good thing I had no plans to settle down or pop out babies. I'd make a horrible wife.

My stomach growled as I pulled out the lunchmeat, mayo, and a loaf of bread from my fridge and assembled a turkey sandwich, cutting the crust off. An old habit from my childhood I'd been unable to curb.

Sandwich in hand, I ate it on my way back to my room, practically swallowing each bite whole. Finishing off the last few bites, I crawled into my bed, unconcerned by the crumbs now dotting my olive green comforter. I'd shake them off come morning and probably make myself another sandwich for breakfast.

Curling into myself under the covers, I closed my eyes and allowed sleep to pull me down into its warm embrace, doing my best not to think about the sexy new neighbor who was probably bad news.

The good-looking ones always were.

Chapter Five

The light began to fade from his eyes as I crawled across the floor in an effort to reach my Papa. My fingertips were raw and bloody as I struggled to carry myself closer to him, digging into the rough wooden floors with each drag of my body.

"I'm coming," I panted in between breaths. I choked on the smoke filling the room, my eyes watering. "Just hang on, Papa. I'm coming."

Another pull across the floor. Glass and debris dug into the soft underside of my arms, causing me to hiss in pain, but I pushed onward, my left leg dragging uselessly behind me.

I woke gasping for breath, drenched in a cold sweat, clutching the hilt of my dagger as if my life depended on it.

"It was just a nightmare," I told myself, though that did little to ease the ache in my chest over the remembered pain.

I miss you so much.

I clenched my leg muscles, confirming that they still worked, and rubbed my hands over my face. I pushed back the wet, loose tendrils of hair that had escaped my braid during my fitful rest and had just returned my dagger to its resting place under my pillow when my senses registered the smell of smoke.

Shit!

I scanned the room, frantically looking for the source.

"You have got to be kidding me!"

I untangled my body from the sheets, tripping and falling into a heap on the floor before I was able to crawl out of my covers and retrieve an old T-shirt. I frenziedly swatted at the bedroom curtains with the T-shirt, but the flames continued to rise.

There was no other choice but to rip the curtains from the window. Flames licked my fingers as I ran to the kitchen.

I threw the curtains into the sink, turned the faucet on full blast, and watched as the water quickly snuffed out the flames. The curtains were ruined.

Turning the water off, I slid down the smooth wooden cabinets until my butt met the cold tile floor.

I folded my arms across my knees and rested my forehead against them. Closing my eyes, I took several deep breaths. My heart raced from the effects of the recurring nightmare.

This was getting out of hand. Up until a week ago, I hadn't had a nightmare in close to a year. But Daniel's death was bringing them back with a vengeance. I needed to get a handle on them before I burned my apartment down. Again.

I missed my parents, but it'd been over six years now. They weren't coming back, and I needed to let it go. My subconscious needed to let it go, and I needed to let Daniel's death go. Not the case, no, I wouldn't let that go. But his death was affecting me in ways I couldn't allow to continue.

I sat on the floor and breathed deeply to calm my nerves. I was beginning to feel chilly from the fine sheen of sweat on my skin, but I was too tired to get up and do anything about it. Every muscle in my body ached. The clock above the stove read 4:00 a.m. I'd slept a solid twelve hours, but it didn't seem to have done much good.

I grabbed hold of the Formica counter and pulled myself up

off the floor. Sliding my hands over to the edge of the sink, I braced my arms there and stared at the ruined mess of curtains. Grabbing the sopping mess of fabric, I pulled out the trash bin from underneath the counter. They made a wet plop when they hit the bottom, but squeezing out the moisture before tossing them in the trash was more effort than I was willing to put into it.

I quietly closed the cabinet door and made my way back to my room. I stripped off the yoga pants and tank top I'd been wearing and retrieved new clothing before padding into the attached bathroom. I set the clothes on the vanity and winced when I caught sight of my reflection in the mirror above. "Damn, you look like hell," I told my reflection.

Cupping my hands, I splashed cool water on my face, not bothering to close my eyes. The cold water was refreshing against my skin. I wasn't in the mood to shower, but once I stepped under the warm spray, I'd feel better. Rather than risk using my pyrokinetic abilities, I waited for the water to heat on its own. After what I'd just gone through, my concentration was crap, and I didn't need to melt the pipes.

After wiping the fog from the mirror, I deftly plaited my dark brown hair.

I stared at my reflection for several minutes and toyed with the end of my braid.

I had my mother's rich brown hair, but our similarities ended there. My eyes were golden brown where hers had been a striking hazel. My complexion, more olive like my papa's, while hers had been a milky white, and my locks were smooth and straight. Hers had cascaded in curls around her shoulders.

I tugged on my braid. I should just cut it. It was the logical thing to do, but I never seemed able to bring myself to follow through.

I remembered my papa chiding me as a teenager over my

hair. "Just the thing for an attacker to grab hold of!" he'd scold during our sparring matches.

But my mother had loved my hair. She'd brushed it every night for me while growing up. I could still feel the phantom touch of her delicate fingers when I thought of her. Every little girl remembers her mother brushing her hair.

We weren't so close in the end. Something had started to drive a wedge in our relationship that I could never put my finger on. When I looked back, I wished I could have figured it out and fixed it.

It sucked knowing she was gone and my hair was all I had left to remind me that she had, in fact, loved me.

Shaking the memories away, I left the bathroom. I was exhausted, but wide-awake, and knew sleep would elude me. I might as well do something productive. I sheathed my daggers and carefully secured them at my hips before shrugging into my leather jacket and pulling on my boots. I made sure to lock my front door securely and gave the other doors on my floor a passing glance, wondering which one Inarus had moved into.

If I had to bet, I'd say it was the one directly across the hall from mine. I didn't know why, but something about it felt different. An energy of sorts that called to my fire.

I shook off the feeling. "You're reading way too much into nothing." I jogged down the four flights of stairs to the street.

Did it matter what apartment he inhabited?

Maybe later today I'd ask to borrow a cup of sugar. Get to know my new neighbor a little bit.

I snorted. Yeah. Like that was going to happen.

Chapter Six

My boot-clad feet thudded against the wet pavement as I jogged to Hills Fitness Center, a short four miles from my apartment complex. My lungs burned with the exertion and reminded me that I wasn't in as good of shape as I'd like. Something I definitely planned to work on.

The fresh air helped to clear my head and shake away the remnants of my nightmare. There were more important things to worry about than my past.

Like maybe a devilishly handsome neighbor.

"Down girl," I told myself. If he was devilishly handsome, then the devil probably wanted him back, because that man had bad news written all over him.

The crisp fall breeze stung my cheeks as I turned the final corner leading to the gym. At the door, I entered in the six-digit lock code and waited for the light to turn green before opening it, grateful James had given me his entry code. Having a friend who owned a gym had its benefits. After-hours access and free membership being two of them.

I enjoyed training when no one else was around to watch. It allowed me to really hit it hard, without worrying about what others would read into it. You could never be too careful these days. To any outsider, I was a human, and I liked to keep up that appearance whenever possible so as not to draw any unwanted attention.

Being a pyrokinetic didn't give me inhuman strength or speed, but it did give me an accelerated healing ability and fire-power, of course.

Not bothering to turn on any of the lights, I used my memory as a guide to avoid stumbling into any equipment. I walked on silent feet towards the back of the gym and headed down an unassuming stairwell that led to the lower level, shedding my coat along the way.

At the base of the stairs, I flicked on the lights and illuminated the large space. Before me stood the gym's open training room. Each wall lined with a variety of weapons. Everything from swords and axes to maces and scimitars.

Some were more for decoration than actual use, but the room reminded me of home nonetheless. My papa had been a weapons collector, though his collection was much smaller than James's.

I ran my fingers along the hilt of several swords to my left before finally selecting a talwar—a Persian sabre with a wickedly curved edge that ran thirty-three inches in length with a six-inch hilt.

I tested its weight in my right hand and judged it to be around forty-seven or forty-eight ounces. It was crafted to be a thrusting sword, a blade meant to kill in a single strike with deadly precision. With my weapon of choice in hand, I headed to the center of the mat and faced off with my imaginary opponent.

I closed my eyes, and I pictured an enemy on an open battlefield. The breeze whistled in my ears and the scent of freshly cut grass tickled my nose. Taking the time to visualize the scene made it that much more real, and in this moment, I had every intention of slaying my demons.

Far away from the gym, I inhaled another lungful of air, then opened my eyes and thrust the sabre in a fluid motion. I followed through with my strike while moving my feet to the left and twisting my shoulders to bring the sabre back for a second strike to my opponent's back, coming from my right.

I repeated the movement several times until my body remembered the steps without conscious thought.

Sweat dripped from my brow as I changed up my movements and reversed my strikes.

Thirty minutes went by and my confidence in my ability to strike a would-be assailant from either angle rose. I began to parry and thrust, alternating directions. Left then right. Right then left.

I mixed my directions even further. Right, right, left. Left, right, left, and then right, left, right. Changing directions until no pattern remained.

Time blurred, no longer relevant in the haze of my imaginary battle. I was covered in sweat. My clothes stuck to the curves of my body like a second skin and my breathing was labored as I struggled to catch my breath.

"Get it together, Ari—" I muttered under my breath.

I decided to give it one more round despite the fatigue plaguing my muscles and made a swift thrust to my right, digging in my heel, when all of a sudden my gaze caught a dark shadow in the corner of the room.

My forward momentum came to an abrupt stop, and I lowered my sword. My heart pounded in my chest, and I caught the familiar steel-colored gaze of the man wrapped in the shadows of a dark corner. Dressed in a faded black tee and black denim jeans paired with matching boots, he looked predatory as he lurked in the darkened corner of the room.

I winced when I lifted my arm to wipe the sweat from my forehead with the hem of my shirt. The dull ache in my neck and shoulders from the vigorous workout told me I'd been down here for a while.

"I thought we were meeting up later?" I placed the talwar back in its resting place along the wall and watched James all but melt out of the shadows.

He made a look at his non-existent watch, then quirked his brow at me. "It is later," he said, his voice thick like honey along my senses.

"Right." I took a seat on the bench next to my jacket. James tossed me a bottle of water. Not bothering to question where he'd conjured it from, I twisted off the cap and drank half its contents in one long pull.

"Thanks." I sniffed and got a whiff of myself. Phew. I did not smell like sunshine and roses today. I silently prayed James hadn't picked up on my B.O. but with shifter senses, that was unlikely.

"No problem." He shrugged and I could see his nose twitch before a slight smile crossed his features.

Damn.

"So just how much later is it now? I seem to have lost track of time down here."

James stepped closer to stand about six feet in front of me. Looking down at me from his high vantage point, he said, "A little after eight. I stopped by your apartment before heading here. When I knocked and you didn't answer, I figured this was your most likely destination."

I nodded. The gym was practically my second home. I came by on an almost daily basis. Sometimes multiple times in the same day. The smell of sweat and leather was comforting and reminded me of the home I'd lost.

Dammit. I'd come here precisely to put away my demons. Not bring them back to the surface. Looking for a way to squelch the desperation that was suddenly rising in the pit of my stomach, I eyed James up and down.

"Puppy wanna play?" I quirked a brow and waited for his reaction.

The frown on James's face told me he didn't find me at all funny. That was okay, because I usually found myself hilarious.

"Shouldn't we head over to meet with the Blackmores?"

All work and no play made me a really moody partner. Not that I voiced that thought aloud.

Instead, I shrugged my shoulders. "We don't have an appointment, so it makes no difference. Besides, they're grieving. I doubt they'll be going anywhere."

He seemed to ponder it for a few minutes. I was sore, and if it was already eight in the morning, that meant I'd been down here for close to three hours. But a sparring session with James was something I'd never turn down. He was one of the few who could give me a real run for my money. Though given that my past sparring partners were strictly human, that wasn't exactly saying much.

I tilted my head from left to right trying to loosen my muscles and popped my neck in the process.

"You going soft on me?" I asked when James remained silent. "If you're too tired, I understand. Maybe you should go back to bed, and I can pick you up around noon. I know how you like your beauty sleep. Like I said, the Blackmores aren't going anywhere."

I was goading him. Not the smartest thing to do to a werewolf, but despite my vigorous workout, my nightmare still weighed heavily on me, and I needed an outlet.

Taking one last swig from my water bottle, I rose from my seat and walked towards him. I stopped just inches away with an arrogant lift to my lips.

"Terms?" I asked. He hadn't agreed. Yet. But he hadn't said no, either, so I had a chance.

James rolled his shoulders and turned his head from side to side. Gotcha!

"Up to you," he said.

I knew he wouldn't pass this up. "No weapons, no claws."

"Ah, you're no fun."

I shrugged, unconcerned. While a sword against James was almost a necessity, it would give him the advantage of shifting, and I was definitely not up for James in his wolf or between form —a mix of human and wolf. A daunting and ridiculously formidable sight. Being a shifter alone would give James a huge advantage in the strength department. But at least in his human form he was less likely to tear me in two.

"No fire, then," James added.

That was fine by me. I might be fireproof, but that didn't mean I had a death wish. I wouldn't risk lighting anything up in an indoor space knowing that the building could collapse, thus killing me.

Fireproof did not equal immortal. I'd learned that the hard way.

The ache between my shoulder blades was making me stiff. I inhaled deeply and exhaled through my nose. I pushed the slight pain in my muscles out of my consciousness. Pulling in several more deep breaths, I squared my shoulders and faced James. I waited for him to strike first, as he was doing with me. But eventually, James's patience ran out, and he lunged. His arms were outstretched as he reached to grab hold of my shoulders. Twisting to the left, I sidestepped his reach while jamming an elbow deep into the center of his back before I quickly stepped out of reach once again.

James turned and liquid silver filled his gaze.

The wolf was coming out to play. This could get interesting.

I grinned and gave him a come and get me wave. James let out a bark of laughter before lunging again, this time coming in low, aiming for my stomach.

I launched myself into the air, narrowly missing his attack, and threw myself over him, rolling to my feet once my body hit the mat.

I wasn't fast enough. As soon as my feet touched the floor, my body was propelled backward as James tossed me over his shoulder. Sonova—

I tucked in my knees and allowed the momentum to turn me in the right direction. My body landed in a low crouch several feet away. The impact jolted through me in a sting of pain that began in the heels of my feet and reached up to my chest.

I heaved out a breath and swept the hair that had escaped my braid out of my face. The ache between my shoulders quickly blossomed into a full-on throbbing sensation. One I was having a difficult time ignoring. Standing up slowly, I strode to my right, watching James through narrowed eyes as he did the same.

This time, I attacked first. I faked a punch to his left flank before changing direction at the last possible second and striking him in the midsection. My knuckles popped and cracked as they met the hard steel of his abdomen. But I ignored the slight pain and landed a left hook to his jaw.

His head snapped back, but only for a second before he was on me, his full weight holding me down against the firm mat. Arching my back, I attempted to twist to my left in an effort to dislodge him. He held firm.

I jerked my head forward. But before my head could connect with his face, he pulled back just enough to avoid my blow.

I squirmed beneath him, already aware that it was no use.

When James began to chuckle, I halted all movement and glared up at him. His eyes glowed, a beautiful metallic quality much like mercury.

If I could just get my hand free, I could gouge out one of those pretty orbs.

James had a wolfish grin on his face. Bastard thought he'd won.

"What are you so damn happy about?"

"I won."

I heaved as my lungs struggled for air under his weight. "You did not win," I gritted out. "This isn't over." I struggled some more and redoubled my efforts.

"Oh, sweetheart, it's over." He settled his weight more firmly against me. His body was like a lead blanket covering mine.

My chest was on fire, my struggles more erratic in my attempt to escape. It felt like a truck was parked on my chest.

James seemed oblivious to my struggles until I heard him cough, his grip on my arms suddenly tightening and his body holding very, very still.

"Um, hey, Ari. You might want to stop doing that." His voice took on an unusual, husky quality.

I ignored him and continued to squirm beneath him. I could break his hold dammit. I could do this.

"You did not win." Defeat was not an option. Hell, I was tempted to cheat and just light his ass on fire.

"Ari, seriously. You need to … stop." He growled deep in his chest. And that's when I felt it. James's body was hard against mine, unyielding. But what had me frozen in place wasn't just his growl, or the weight of his body on top of me. It was the hard length of him pressed against my lower stomach.

Shit! I glared at him.

"Really, James?!" He thought now was a good time to get horny? Weren't men supposed to have developed some level of control once they passed their teenage years?

"Hey, I'm a guy. You can only expect so much from me."

Excuses, excuses.

He grinned, and I had the sudden urge to smack him upside the head. If only I could get my arm free. Right now I did not need my hormones getting the wrong idea, and my nether bits were starting to tingle. Yeah, they were definitely getting the wrong idea.

"You going to get off of me?" I asked, rolling my eyes at his pleased expression.

In one fluid movement, James was off me and standing

several feet away. He didn't bother trying to hide the bulge between his legs, and at first, I didn't bother trying not to notice. But then reality hit. This was James.

I smoothed out the non-existent wrinkles in my shirt and readjusted my braid before standing up. Going for casual. Nothing strange happening here. My thighs were not instinctively tightening nor was my heart pounding in my chest at the prospect of having sex. Hot, delicious, sex. Nope.

"Umm, you ready to get moving?" I asked, avoiding eye contact.

James began to laugh, a deep rumble that caused me to jerk my head in his direction.

"God, Ari, you are such a prude."

"I am not!" I snapped. I folded my arms across my chest. If only he knew the thoughts going through my head right now. Thank God he didn't.

Still rocking his shit-eating grin he rolled his eyes. "Yeah, riiiight. Why don't you go shower while I clean up here."

I nodded and started to head towards the showers. "Better yet, I could join you," his voice deepened. He wiggled his eyebrows suggestively, and I felt my mouth drop open.

Was he kidding? He had to be kidding.

James and I were in the friend zone. The unwavering friend zone.

My stomach clenched. Come on. Get it together.

James folded over and held his stomach, laughing so hard tears leaked from his eyes. "God, if you could see the look on your face," he said between gasping breaths.

I whirled away and stomped the rest of the way towards the locker room. I had to walk past him, but managed to keep my head held high and my eyes straight-forward. When I was only inches away from James, I gripped his bicep and, bending my knees, pulled him over my shoulder as I tucked my body in.

James sailed through the air and, caught off guard, landed in an ungraceful heap a few feet away.

He turned to me, a shocked smile on his face and a glint in his eyes. "You fight dirty." He said it as though it were a compliment.

I continued on my way, not bothering to look back. "Try not to forget it."

Chapter Seven

I took a cold shower. It'd been too long since I'd been with anyone, but the last thing I needed was my mind straying to James. Dry spell or not, he was off limits.

This was all the sexy new neighbor's fault. I'd had no problem keeping my libido in check until he came along.

Yeah. I was going to blame all of this on him.

I didn't have many friends, and I couldn't afford to ruin one of my few friendships just to get laid.

I sighed. It'd be a hell of a lot easier for my mind not to stray to the feel of his body against mine, his length pressed against my abdomen, if he wasn't so damn good looking.

No, Aria, just no.

I stepped out of the tile enclosure and quickly dried off. I threw on a spare set of clothes I kept in a locker—black yoga pants and a shirt that said, *some people just need a high five … in the face … with a chair,* and re-plaited my hair, silently cursing my damn hormones. James was practically my brother. He was my go-to person second only to Mike. I fiddled with the leather bracelet around my wrist as I walked to the lobby to wait for him.

We had boundaries. Boundaries were good.

I looked over my shoulder when I heard a door open and watched James stalk toward me. The dark brown hair, chiseled abs, and steely grey eyes made him one fine specimen. He exuded sex appeal.

I groaned.

He could easily walk into a bar and have his choice of any woman in there. *He's like a brother, Aria,* I reminded myself. Albeit a hot brother, a brother, nonetheless. Maybe more like a stepbrother. I shook myself again. Hard.

It didn't matter. Relationships were fleeting, and our friendship was something I'd never risk so carelessly.

"You ready to get going?" His lips curved as he waited for my response.

The response I had yet to voice, because I was standing there like an idiot, staring at the black T-shirt molded to his perfect chest.

I swallowed, my mouth suddenly dry. "Yeah, I'm ready," I finally croaked.

I followed James up the stairs and through the gym as he led the way to the parking lot. The doors to the Mustang unlocked with a distinct click, and I climbed in the passenger side. After securing my seatbelt, I relaxed into the plush leather seat.

We rode in silence to the Blackmore residence. I was too exhausted from our sparring session to make any conversation. But, if I were being entirely honest, every time I went to say something, he'd glance my way with a sly smile, and I'd clam up and turn away, pretending to find something outside interesting.

He chuckled under his breath.

Fifteen long minutes later, we pulled up to the Blackmore residence, a charming three-story house. James left the engine running for a few moments while we each surveyed the neighborhood through the car's tinted windows. The home was beautifully landscaped with those bushes people liked to groom into spires and little fairy statues scattered throughout the rose-filled flower beds. Honestly, plants that needed a haircut every week weren't worth the effort in my book. Though it seemed to be the expectation in neighborhoods like this.

The Blackmore house was your typical Veradale home. Narrow and tall with three stories and gingerbread trim, it was situated within a gated community that gave the false impression of safety. One of those cookie cutter neighborhoods where all of the houses looked similar, apart from varying paint colors.

The meticulous slate pathway leading to the front door and the detailed molding around the windows screamed expensive.

We climbed out of the Mustang and made our way to the front door. But before I could knock, the door opened. A tall woman dressed in a sleek, green, knee-length dress stood before me. Her hair was impeccable. Styled in a fall of curls down her right shoulder. Large gemstones that looked to be emeralds adorned her ears, and her makeup was flawless against her alabaster complexion.

"Mrs. Blackmore." My mouth gaped open, and I had to remind myself to shut it.

"Yes?"

"We're sorry to bother you," I said by way of greeting. I tried to shake the uncertainty that suddenly coursed through me. "But we wanted to speak with you a little more about Daniel's disappearance and ..." I trailed off. She knew her son was dead. I didn't need to remind her of that.

A small frown creased Jessica's brow, and she looked over her shoulder at the sound of approaching footsteps.

"I'm sorry, but this isn't really a good time. We were just on our way out."

A middle-aged man stepped up beside her. With a jerk of his hand, he forced her to open the door wider.

"Who is it?" he asked in a curt voice, as though he couldn't see me standing right in front of him.

He wasn't blind, was he? I scrutinized his face, but he didn't have the tale tell milky whites of a blind man.

"It's the investigator that was working on Daniel's case. Ms. Ummm …What was your name again?" she asked, turning back towards me, an apologetic expression on her face.

The man glowered down at me. Nope, not blind. Just an asshole.

"Aria. Aria Naveed." Obviously, I hadn't made much of an impression on her. Maybe I needed to get myself a Boss 302 Mustang so I could be seen and remembered, too.

"It's Ms. Naveed," she told her husband, even though he'd clearly heard me.

"Why is she here?" he asked distractedly.

Not wanting Mrs. Blackmore to continue playing the middleman, I focused my attention on Patrick Blackmore and answered him directly. "I'm here to discuss the circumstances surrounding Daniel's abduction and murder." I kept my voice even and my expression pleasant as I watched him for any reactions. I wasn't sure what I was looking for, exactly, but something didn't feel right.

"Why? It's over. Done with," he said in a gruff voice as he adjusted the burgundy tie around his thick neck.

I really wanted to pull on it and see if his face would turn the same color. For some reason, I disliked him on sight. He had sleaze ball written all over him, and I wasn't particularly fond of the way he kept eyeing me up and down like some piece of meat.

I gave him a tooth-filled smile and a little bit of crazy eyes. I didn't do well with creepy men leering at me, and if he didn't stop, I wouldn't be held responsible for my actions.

"No, Mr. Blackmore, it isn't over," James said from behind me. He took a menacing step forward, his tone laced with steel.

I corrected my expression, keeping it blank as Mr. and Mrs. Blackmore studied James over my shoulder. I could tell that neither one of them knew who or what he was. If they did, their expressions would have changed from annoyance to apprehension at the very least.

I was surprised by their reaction to my visit though. They had just lost a child. It had only been a matter of weeks since Daniel's disappearance. And news of his death was brought to their attention only a handful of days ago, yet the two of them looked as if they were going out to celebrate.

These weren't the grieving parents I'd expected to meet with this afternoon. Everyone handles grief differently, but their complete lack of emotion was off-putting, to say the least.

"We are Daniel's parents, and we've decided that this case is over," Mr. Blackmore bit out, his patience visibly running out. "Your services are no longer needed."

James grinned. It was a feral smile full of teeth. The kind of smile most would consider friendly, but I knew better. This was the smile James showed people before he smashed their heads into pool tables and bruised every inch of their bodies. I'd seen it a few times over the past few months, and it never ended well for the other guy.

"What about Daniel's biological father?" he said.

Jessica's eyes widened, and her husband's face deepened in color. Hmm … I didn't need to pull on that tie after all.

"Who do you think—"

"Mr. Blackmore, allow me to introduce you to my associate. James Shields."

I could tell that Patrick Blackmore still had no idea who he was, but Jessica did. As soon as I said his name, her skin grew pale. The pulse point in her throat drummed rapidly beneath her skin, her hands clenching and unclenching in an anxious gesture. One she was likely unaware of. She'd been with Eric Delaney long enough to have learned the who's who within the Pack, and I'd put money on the fact that she knew James was the Pack Hunter.

I silently cursed. It seemed everyone had been in the know but me.

"I don't care who you are—" Patrick said before his wife interrupted him.

"Patrick, please." She placed a hand on his folded forearm. He looked down at her in irritation, and I could tell he was about to brush her off. I decided to jump in to keep him from slamming the door in our faces.

It was a very nice door, and I really didn't want to have to kick it down.

"Mr. Blackmore, I believe that your wife is trying to warn you. Because unlike you, she realizes the significance of Mr. Shields' presence. James is a member of the Pacific Northwest Pack. He is here on official Pack business. As I am sure you are well aware, Daniel Blackmore was a shifter. A tidbit of information the two of you failed to provide early on, which means the Pack has every right to investigate his murder, and you, sir, would do best to cooperate. I assure you that it's in your best interest." I said all of this in a sugary sweet voice with a businesslike smile on my face.

I hadn't known that Mrs. Blackmore could go any paler, but she did. Her skin had taken on an ashen quality, and I made a mental note to watch her for any further reactions. There was something very wrong about these two.

Patrick seemed to digest my words. I could tell he was fuming, but he made the smart choice and opened the door wider, letting us in. Looking over my shoulder, I gave James a feral grin of my own and stepped aside to allow him to take the lead. I was slowly growing used to his irrational form of chivalry, so I followed him in without comment, all the while picturing lighting the hem of his shirt on fire.

I whistled softly to myself. It would serve him right.

Mr. and Mrs. Blackmore led us into a sitting room directly to the right of the entryway. Everything in the room—the thick,

Oriental carpets, heavy damask draperies, silk covered sofas—was refined and of quality material. My hands itched around all of this finery. As I lowered myself onto a deep blue love seat, I luxuriated in the feel of the silky fabric, while another completely irrational part of me wanted to light the damn thing on fire.

Being a pyrokinetic was no walk in the park.

Once everyone was seated, we all stared at one another in silence. I honestly had no idea where to begin.

When I'd first met Jessica Blackmore, she was a distraught mother, tear tracks down her face and bruises beneath her eyes. But now … now she looked better than ever. I couldn't wrap my head around the sudden change in her appearance.

I'd never met Peter Blackmore. But a man who easily had ten years on his wife, greasy hair, and a thick midsection, was not who I pictured for Jessica's husband. She was beautiful in a classic way. Like a modern Audrey Hepburn. But after meeting the two together, it was safe to assume that she'd married for money. Times were rough. The Awakening had completely collapsed the economy, so wealth or even comfort were hard to come by for most.

Jessica seemed the type that wanted to be taken care of. I couldn't blame her for that. But I could judge her all I wanted.

Silence hung in the air. Everyone unsure how to break it.

"Did either of you have anything to do with your son's death?" James said.

I raised my brows and stared at him. I'd been thinking along the same lines but hadn't anticipated him actually voicing the question so boldly. Nonetheless, I eyed both parties, waiting for a response. If the tension in the room got any thicker, we'd suffocate.

"Of course not!" Patrick said. His voice rose in outrage.

"No. I would never," Jessica said in a more subdued tone.

James inhaled a deep breath through his nose and tilted his head to the side. He appeared lost in thought for a moment.

Jessica twisted her hands nervously in her lap, and Patrick's face was red with rage. He was on the verge of exploding and was holding onto his temper by the thinnest of threads.

Not that I cared. If either of these two had anything to do with Daniel's death, I would make them suffer, and it wouldn't be pretty.

"You have no right to come into my home and accuse either of us of foul play. We did nothing wrong," Patrick said. He turned to his wife and rested a hand on her shoulder. For a moment I thought he was comforting her, but her eyes flickered with a hint of uncertainty before tears began flowing freely down her face.

The reaction was delayed. She was clearly faking it. But why?

"Now, you've made my wife upset. I'd like you to leave," Blackmore bit out.

James stared at Mrs. Blackmore in silence, his gaze assessing. Every few seconds her gaze would flicker to his before she promptly looked away, her tears increasing. She was putting on quite the show.

I pulled one of my daggers out and began using it to clean my fingernails. Mr. Blackmore eyed my blade with equal parts apprehension and outrage. He wasn't accustomed to being threatened, and he certainly was not used to losing control over a situation. Not that I was openly threatening anyone. At least, not yet.

"Mr. and Mrs. Blackmore," I said, addressing them both. Jessica sniffled a few more times before wiping her face and pulling herself together. I had to give it to her—she was almost convincing. Almost.

"I'd like you to be aware of our investigation and know that we will bring down the individual or individuals responsible for Daniel's murder." I pinned both of them with a hard stare, allowing the meaning of my statement to sink in. If either of them had played any part in their son's death, I'd make them burn for it.

They were supposed to be loving parents. There should be grief over their son's death, not whatever this was.

Abruptly James stood up. "Thank you for your time. We'll show ourselves out."

I gave him a questioning look, but the slight shake of his head kept me from voicing the question out loud. Instead, I stood up, nodded at the two surprised individuals seated across from us, and followed James out the front door, not bothering to say anything else.

Outside, James and I headed straight to the car. Once my seatbelt was buckled he started the engine.

"They were lying, weren't they?" I asked him as he put the car into drive.

"I don't know."

"What do you mean you don't know? I thought shifters could scent a lie?"

"We can," he snarled and ran a hand through his hair. "But something is off about those two. Especially the mother. My wolf is fighting to get out. He's angry and senses a wrongness in them. I'm not sure what it is. I'm having a difficult time keeping him in." James tightened his hands on the steering wheel as we wove our way through traffic and merged onto the freeway. "They know something. Their lie wasn't outright. It felt more like a lie of omission."

"You can scent a lie of omission?"

James shook his head. "It's more of a feeling. I'm going to put a tail on them and see what that exposes. When they said they weren't involved in Daniel's death, that was the truth. I think. But when Blackmore said they'd done nothing wrong, that was a lie."

Parents loved their kids, right? I didn't have any children, so I had no idea what that was like. But I knew my parents loved me, and I'd thought Jessica loved her son. But that woman back there, she wasn't the mother I'd initially met.

"Do you usually have problems containing your wolf?" I hadn't had the pleasure of seeing James lose control before, but I could see his skin start to ripple and knew a shift was close.

He gave me a sidelong look that said he didn't like my question. I shrugged my shoulders and waited for him to answer anyway. I trusted James completely, but I was really hoping he'd get things under control. The prospect of being locked in a car with a wolf didn't sound so appealing.

"No. I don't have issues containing my wolf. Ever," he ground out.

"Well, you're obviously having issues today. I think you should get a handle on that before you go all furry on me." I gave him a sweet, and what I hoped was an innocent, smile.

He cringed, so much for sweet and innocent.

I lowered the visor mirror and smiled at my reflection.

"What are you doing?"

"Admiring myself." I smiled and then shrank back. It looked forced and a bit crazed. I tried again, this time pulling the corners of my mouth down just a bit.

Oh, not any better. At least I knew I'd mastered crazy.

"Are you smiling at yourself?"

I shut the mirror and put the visor back up before glaring at him. "Yes, I'm smiling at myself. Do you have a problem with that?"

"Seriously, Ari?" he said in a condescending tone.

"I just want to make sure I look normal when I smile, 'kay? Can we move on now?"

James started laughing, a deep rumble in his chest, and I had to grit my teeth and cross my arms to keep from smacking him upside the head.

Idiot.

Chapter Eight

Today was going to be one of those days where even my coffee needed a cup of coffee. Thankfully, after saying as much, James relented and drove me by the local Rocket Bakery down the street from my office. If he'd learned anything from working with me, it was that the most dangerous drinking game you could play with me was seeing how long I could go without having a cup. I drank coffee like a Gilmore Girl and trust me when I tell you, no one wanted to see how long I could go without.

With a steaming cup of deliciousness in my hands, I rested my booted feet on the edge of my desk and inhaled the earthy aroma, allowing the warm steam to fill my senses.

Come to momma.

Taking a tentative sip, I let the thick, warm liquid make its way down my throat before returning for a steaming gulp.

I moaned. It was that good.

James sat across from my desk in the guest chair with his own cup of coffee. I watched through half-closed lids as he took several deep gulps, devouring the beverage in a matter of seconds. I shook my head. He didn't even taste it. What a waste.

"Do you always chug your coffee?" I asked.

"How else am I supposed to get the stuff down?"

I stared at him through hooded eyes. "What do you mean, 'get it down?' Don't you like it?"

James made a face of disgust. "Nope. I can barely stand the stuff."

"Then why do you drink it?" I was starting to reconsider our friendship. How could anyone who didn't drink coffee be sane?

He shrugged his broad shoulders. "Dunno, for the caffeine kick I guess."

"You don't get a caffeine kick. The Lyc-V in your system burns through it too quickly to get any sort of result." Lyc-V, short for the lycanthropy virus, attached itself to each string of DNA in its host's body, mutating the cells to create a hybrid between man and beast.

The virus was virulent and infected the host through their blood, but it had its perks, too. I'd say getting an increased metabolism, strength, speed, and increased sensitivity to sound were a pretty decent trade off. A downside though was that no, you didn't get any caffeine kicks.

"If I drink enough of it, I guess I can get a caffeine buzz for a minute. Maybe two." James's gaze was far away for a moment. "Maybe thirty espresso shots. Maybe more." He shrugged.

"Okay, so again, why do you drink it?"

James shrugged again.

I was getting nowhere. "If you don't drink coffee, I'm not sure we can be friends."

James grinned, and my lady bits decided to come to attention. *Down, girl. Down.*

"Why do you think I'm drinking it?" He raised his empty cup in a mock salute.

"Whatever," I mumbled under my breath as I savored the remainder of my cup of joe. "I'm not buying you coffee anymore."

A man crossed the front office window and came to a stop at the street corner, catching my attention. I leaned forward to get a better look, ignoring James as he looked around the office. The man kept his head low. A hoodie covered most of his face. He managed to angle himself away enough so I couldn't make out anything distinguishable, but I had the distinct impression that his attention was directed inside my office.

The hairs on the back of my neck stood. The front office window was open at the street level, and when I'd arrived, I'd opened the blinds to let some light in. Now I was beginning to second guess that decision.

The glint of silver in the man's left hand caught my attention, but just as I rose from my seat, he turned and began to cross the street.

I stared at the window, unable to shake the feeling that whoever he was, he wasn't a friendly.

Forcing my gaze away, I turned to watch James's study of the office.

It was a decent sized room sectioned off into four office spaces, a small kitchen, and three side rooms. One was used to catch some sleep, another housed weapons, and the third was a small bathroom. There was a small apartment above the office that I'd lived in before getting a place of my own, but it'd been over a year since anyone had occupied it.

The main office space housed mine and Mike's desks along with a large L-shaped desk that Nico and Taylor shared when they were around. They were a team and chose to be side by side both in and out of the office.

There were two small folding tables pushed off into a corner for the non-regulars to use as a desk should they need a workspace and a small collection of worn metal-framed office chairs like the ones you'd see in a doctors office.

It wasn't much, but it did the job well enough.

James walked slowly around the perimeter of the room,

examining the various article clippings and pictures framed on the walls. Mike was a tad sentimental and liked to document anything that he considered to be a memorable event.

Most of the images were from solved cases—missing people who were found, lives that were saved in the nick of time. Those faded clippings were our Hall of Fame. The reason we showed up each morning. Sure, we were mercs, but we had hearts.

I just wished Daniel Blackmore's image could have made its way onto that wall.

"So, what do you suggest we do next?" James asked from across the room.

I raised an eyebrow at his question, surprised he was letting me take the lead.

"First, arrange a meeting with the Coven. Daniel's death was at the hands of a vampire. Now that the Pack is involved, they'll be more willing to cooperate than they were before."

"Why would you think that?"

"Well, it would be in their best interest to avoid a war, wouldn't it? And the death of a shifter child could easily ignite one. I think, if given all of the proper facts, Rebecka will realize it's better to just hand over the perpetrator than to have us dig further. Politics and all that nonsense."

Rebecka was the local vampire Coven leader. From what I'd gathered, she wouldn't bat an eyelash over hanging one of her own out to dry if it benefitted her, and she wouldn't hesitate to throw one to the wolves if it kept her Coven safe. "Besides, if the culprit is a rogue vampire, we'd be doing her a favor."

"I think you're wrong, Ari," he said, his tone now grim.

"And why is that?" I thought over my earlier statement, and it still sounded solid in my mind. If they could get farther in life, or the afterlife, by severing their own hand, they would do it.

"The vampires want a war. They've slowly been growing their numbers and believe they're in a position to challenge the Pack for power over the territory as a whole. They want us out, completely."

"The Pack has what, a couple thousand shifters within the Pacific Northwest? The Coven doesn't have a chance. Besides, don't the Pack and the Coven have a truce of sorts?"

"We do, which is why they haven't shown any outright aggression, but this—this is something that, like you said, can ignite a war. When it boils down to just numbers, we have them over the Coven nearly five to one if we pulled everyone in, but that would include our vulnerable. Of those who can fight, we outnumber the vampires two to one instead. I know how Rebecka's mind works. We've been studying her habits and tracing back through her history for years. She wouldn't plan a takeover if she didn't think she could win. That is what concerns us the most."

James shook his head in frustration.

I hadn't realized the Pack was keeping tabs on the Coven, let alone tracing Rebecka's history, but it made sense. A truce was made for a reason, and while the hope was usually to build long-lasting political relationships, the reality was that they were enacted simply to keep everyone from killing each other. There was always a reason that they wanted to kill each other. Not that those reasons always made sense.

Chapter Nine

Forty minutes. Forty minutes on hold, listening to I don't even know what—music from way before my time—being shuffled from one unhelpful vampire to another, but I'd finally secured an appointment to meet with Rebecka at eleven tonight. I knew damn well they were jerking my chain with all the runaround, but that was the way of vampires.

Especially Rebecka. The Cove—the vampire's not so secret hidey hole—was an old historic building built in 1901 that boasted eclectic architecture and beautiful landscaping. Before all things paranormal came out, the Cove had been used by a non-profit organization. Rooms had often been rented out for events and tours had been offered to the public. From what I'd learned, Rebecka and the rest of the local vampires began occupying the mansion about five years ago, shortly after the Awakening.

Where they had lived before, no one knew, but they were here now, and I doubted they would be moving any time soon.

Now it was rare for any non-vampire to ever enter the establishment. Vampires couldn't enter homes without being invited, but since the mansion had no permanent residents, vampires were able to come and go as they pleased. But they were a bit touchy about uninvited guests. I always assumed since they weren't able to enter the homes of others, they didn't want others coming into theirs.

It made sense in a twisted, jealous sort of way.

At 10:55 p.m., James and I pulled up to the elegant mansion nestled south of Upriver Drive. Small pockets of light glowed between shrubs and stones, lighting the sweeping lawn and its rich, lush grass. Even though it was dark out, every piece of molding and every detail in the stained glass windows could be seen. It was breathtaking.

I hadn't realized I was staring until I heard James slam shut the driver's side door. Clearing my head, I followed suit and exited the Mustang. James came around and stopped beside me as we both gazed ahead. Taking a deep breath, I pushed back my shoulders and took measured steps up the stone pathway with James by my side.

The temperature had dropped once the sun went down, and I wished I'd taken the time to add an extra layer beneath my leather jacket. The moon hung high in the sky and illuminated the street around us.

It was eerily quiet. No sounds of traffic, no insects chirping. Just endless silence that had my nerves on edge. I casually brushed my hands along the handles of my daggers, hanging low on my hips in their leather sheaths.

Their soft weight added an extra measure of comfort as I headed straight into unknown territory. I told myself I was walking into a lion's den, but really, this was far worse. With lions, they at least still had a heart.

When we reached the front door, I admired the woodwork once more before administering three solid knocks.

James and I waited in silence as the distinct sound of high heels on wood flooring grew progressively louder.

The door opened on silent hinges to reveal the most beautiful woman I had ever seen. She towered over me by a good five inches, with a figure most women would die for—thin, but not too thin, wide hips, narrow waist, curves in all the right places. Wearing a floor-length navy dress, she looked like a movie star, if such things still existed after the Awakening.

"Follow me," she said in a cultured voice.

James and I stepped over the threshold and followed at an appropriate distance. I flicked my gaze at each doorway we passed, waiting for the boogeyman to jump out at me. When he didn't, I forced myself to relax and turned my attention to the woman's long red hair that cascaded down her back. The color was striking but most likely came from a box. It was too vivid to be natural.

Her heels clicked on the hardwood floors as we made our way to the main sitting room in the home. Dragging my gaze away from her, I looked around to admire the beauty that was the Cove while also taking inventory of all exits. Every vampire here was a potential threat, so having more than one escape route was a necessity.

The entryway appeared to have its original floors and woodwork. The craftsmanship was beautiful, and the rich beams on the ceiling were hard not to appreciate. The hall was devoid of windows, though, and none of the doorways we passed looked like an exterior door.

The beautiful cream and gold wallpaper dotted with accents of red were rather remarkable next to all of the deep rich woods and plush draperies. The draperies had likely been relined to block out the sun during daylight hours. All of the light fixtures looked original as well. It didn't appear that Rebecka had made any modifications upon acquiring the mansion, which was to my benefit since I knew the layout from having visited it when it was open to the public.

There was a reason that legend said vampires couldn't go out in the sun, and they were almost right about why. The truth of the matter was that newer vampires were able to withstand the sun's harsh rays for longer since their bodies contained more moisture. It had to do with the lack of water contained in their bodies after the change and the sun causing extreme dehydration at an accelerated rate.

If they'd been undead for fewer than five years, they could typically withstand sun exposure for anywhere from thirty minutes to an hour, as long as it wasn't direct. Any older and a vampire's skin would begin to wither. If they were out for more than a minute or two, they would die.

I'd seen a vampire die from sun exposure. Several years ago, when I was visiting Seattle, Washington, the local Coven decided to make a demonstration. I wasn't sure what the crime had been, but the Coven tied a vampire to a post in the middle of Pike Place Market with silver infused chains and left him for dead. He'd struggled aimlessly to free himself and pleaded with onlookers to help. But no one was willing to risk the Coven's wrath to save him.

When dawn came, and the sun began to rise, the vampire's skin began to boil and blister. Within minutes his body withered to a dry husk. Within an hour, he deteriorated further, and nothing but ash remained. It was a ghastly sight, and the stench of burnt, rotting flesh was one I'd never forget.

We made our way out of the entryway and up three small steps into the parlor. The room was just as beautiful as the previous one, but much lighter. The walls were a buttery cream and the ceiling heavily adorned with hand-painted scroll-like patterns.

The fire beneath my skin came to attention at the sight of Rebecka. A reminder that we were in the presence of a very real threat. I took a deep breath and urged my fire to remain calm. After some effort, the flames inside of me subsided, and the temperature in the room visibly dropped.

James gave me a concerned glance, but I chose to ignore it.

Rebecka sat in a Victorian-era chaise near the fireplace, a

small leather-bound book in her hands. She conveyed the image of beauty and serenity. Both of which I knew to be complete fallacies. Rebecka was a cold hearted, malicious bitch. The beauty she showed on the outside disguised the ugliness within.

Dressed in a floor-length cream silk dress with her blonde hair pulled back in an elegant updo, curls tumbling around her face, she looked as if she were born in the Victorian era. For all I knew, she had been. There was always an air of sophistication about her despite her youthful, almost child-like appearance. She sat with a stillness that only a vampire could achieve, not bothering to make the minute movements, like blinking her eyes, that would set most non-vampires at ease. I knew she'd heard our arrival, enhanced vampire senses and all, but she ignored our presence, keeping her focus on the book in her hands.

James and I stood in silence, waiting for her to deign to acknowledge us, while the woman who'd led us here made her way closer to Rebecka. It was never a good idea to interrupt a vampire. Their tempers were fickle things, and I knew her blatant disregard for our presence was simply a power play to assert control over the meeting.

Real mature, right? You'd think that after hundreds of years she'd have learned to play nice.

After several long seconds had passed, Rebecka placed the worn book on the empty seat beside her and rose to her full height next to the fireplace. The warm glow cast small shadows across her face. Vampires were notoriously afraid of fire. I was surprised she had chosen to light a fire in the first place, let alone stand so close to it.

Another tactic perhaps? Something to show she was afraid of nothing. Or I could just be reading too much into it. I always wondered if Vampires were like reptiles with their cold blood and inability to warm themselves. Their skin was always cool to the touch. Unable to lay out in the sun's warming rays, maybe the fire offered some semblance of comfort?

"Irina, what a pleasant surprise it is to have the Pack Hunter and his human companion grace our humble home," she said in a sweet, musical voice.

She wasn't fooling me one bit.

The woman beside her, Irina, offered a tight nod. Her welcoming demeanor now shut off since she didn't have to play guide anymore. She didn't look the least bit pleased by our presence.

I guess James's status as Hunter wasn't such a secret after all. How the hell had everyone else known he was the Hunter and I hadn't?

"Thank you for seeing us on such short notice," I replied. My hands itched to pull out my blades, but I kept them firmly at my sides. If I attacked Rebecka, there wasn't a chance in hell that I would leave the Cove alive.

Rebecka's assessing gaze quickly swept over me before she turned away, having decided I wasn't worth her attention. That was the thing about vampires—they were always so self-absorbed. So assured of their own power and abilities that humans like myself didn't even register on their radar.

That was okay. I was just fine letting her believe I was nothing more than a weak human, even if it did chafe at my pride.

James stood vigilant beside me. I'd expected him to step forward and take the conversational lead after Rebecka's obvious dismissal of me, but he remained silent and still as a statue though his eyes flickered from liquid mercury to smoky grey faster than my eyes could track.

His wolf wasn't happy to be here.

James was positioned exactly one step behind me and slightly to my left, almost as if he were standing guard. As silence hung in the air, I watched Rebecka's lips thin in irritation. A very telling sign on a vampire, since in most cases their patience was near endless.

"Are you not going to speak, dog?" Rebecka said, disgust in

her tone.

James remained silent, but I noticed the slight shift of his weight behind me.

Without putting too much thought into it, I raised my chin and stared Rebecka straight in the eyes. "Actually, you'll be speaking with me." I took several steps forward towards the nearby lounge chair. "Do you mind if I have a seat?" Not waiting for a response, I sat down in the velvet covered chair, crossed my legs, and leaned back as if I didn't have a care in the world.

I heard a barely audible hiss come from Irina's direction but didn't bother looking her way. Power was all about perception, and I wasn't going to let these two see me squirm.

I felt, more than heard, James come up beside me, but I kept my complete focus on Rebecka. The tension in the room seemed to shoot skywards, but I paid it no mind. I had long ago perfected a look of disinterest while on the streets. I learned early on that information was power, but it was reckless to let people know you were looking for it. I would learn more if I acted like I really didn't give two shits.

"So," I began, effectively breaking the silence and cracking the thick veil of tension in the room. "We've come to request the Coven's cooperation in a case involving a shifter child that was murdered by a Coven member."

"No Coven members have committed such a crime," Irina said through clenched teeth. I knew that would get a response.

My gaze flickered in her direction before returning to Rebecka, effectively telling Irina how little her opinion mattered in this conversation. If it were possible for the undead to flush, I'd imagine that Irina's complexion would be scarlet with rage. As it was, I could practically see steam coming out of her ears and had to fight back a smile. I didn't know her, so I shouldn't really care whether or not I made her angry, but I had little respect for the vampire race as a whole. Pissing off one of Rebecka's minions wasn't beneath me, not in the least.

Actually, there were few lows that I wouldn't stoop to, to get what I wanted.

"And why should the Spokane Coven assist a human and the Pack?" Rebecka sneered the words human and pack. "What benefit does this hold for us?"

"Does the Coven have to benefit in some way in order for you to assist the Pack in bringing a murderer to justice?" I already knew the answer to that question, but it spewed out of my mouth anyway.

"Yes," she said. "We do."

The smug look on Rebecka's face dialed up my outrage, and I saw heat begin to rise in waves from the floor.

"Fine," I said. "How much do you want? Name your price." I knew the Pack would pay almost any dollar amount to get their hands on the bastard responsible for Daniel's death.

Rebecka laughed and a wide grin stole across her features, drawing attention to the twin fangs within her mouth.

"You think you can buy this information? That your money means anything to me? No, dear child, your money means nothing. As Irina said, our Coven had no part in the matter. You may go." She waved her hand, dismissing us.

I stood from my seat. So much for diplomacy. "I'm not going to let this go. You can't protect that son of a bitch forever. Whoever it is, they're going to rot for what they did to that little boy."

I was seething now. A red haze clouded my vision.

A slow smile creep across Rebecka's face. I wanted to slap her.

"We'll see," she said.

James placed a hand on my shoulder and nodded towards the door. I didn't want to leave. I wanted to punch the information out of her smug face, but I knew that wouldn't work.

I wouldn't even make it close to her before I was overwhelmed, and the worry in James's eyes said he knew it and thought I might attack anyway.

I ground my teeth together. My fingernails broke the skin of my palms as I clenched my fists in an effort to contain my rage. My breathing was heavy, and my skin was now hot to the touch. I didn't need to take my own temperature to know that I was well beyond feverish and within boiling range.

Frustration burned through my veins as I stomped out of the room. James stayed close, and we passed several vampires who now lined the hallways, each with exposed fangs and malevolent grins.

I jerked the door handle and felt the brass melt beneath my hands. Shit.

I pulled the handle with all my strength but it wouldn't budge. Seeing my problem, James reached down, and with one quick pull, he broke the handle off and tossed it to me.

Shoving the evidence of my powers into my pocket, we continued down the exterior steps and headed in the direction of James's car.

As we approached the Mustang, I made the swift decision to keep walking. At the moment, I didn't trust myself not to melt the seats or, hell, blow the damn thing up.

James quickly fell in step beside me. As we continued farther down the street, I felt the ripple of heat beneath my skin become stronger. I increased my pace, frantically looking around for any kind of water source. I wasn't going to last much longer.

"You doing okay?" James asked. I could hear the worry in his voice.

I shook my head, beyond the ability to speak.

James reached for my hand. When his skin touched mine, he hissed in pain and jerked back.

"Christ, Ari! You're on fire."

He rubbed his palm against his jeans and scanned the surrounding area. I looked at my arms and legs as I half walked, half jogged down the street.

What was he talking about? I wasn't on fire yet. But I was getting there.

James took a deep breath through his nose. On his second inhale, he jerked his head towards the right, and I almost slowed to see what had caught his attention.

"Come on. The river is this way."

Thank God!

Nodding, I followed him as he picked up the pace to a steady run. He didn't say anything else, but every few seconds he'd glance over his shoulder in concern.

I desperately needed to release the boiling anger inside of me but I couldn't. It wasn't safe. Not here. Not so close to the Coven.

Sweat dripped down my back between my shoulder blades. I was going to overheat, and that was not a good thing. Inwardly, I cursed. I was never this on edge. What the hell was happening to me?

I tried to focus on James in front of me. His muscles rippled beneath his skin. "You're about to shift."

Liquid mercury met my gaze over his shoulder. "My wolf needs a release after being around so many vampires."

We stopped for a quick moment and James quickly shed his shirt. His back suddenly arched, then distorted as the shift took over his form. I'd seen James shift before, but each time caught my breath.

Fur exploded across his skin. Claws elongated from his fingers, and his face contorted into a grotesque mask before taking the form of a wolf's snout. In a matter of seconds, James was on all fours beside me, his thick black coat glistening in the moonlight.

He took off at a dead run. A pace I had no chance of keeping up with. I followed him anyway. Unable to see him through the dense night but able to hear his howls in the air when he realized I was too far behind.

Finally, the sweet sound of running water caught my

attention, and I ran with every ounce of energy I could muster. I pumped my arms and legs as fast as they would take me. I ignored James in his wolf form as he sat on the rocky shore and bolted straight into the river.

Within seconds the frigid water brought my core temperature down to a manageable level. I sucked in a breath of air and lay back, submerging my entire body under the clear surface.

I closed my eyes and focused all of my efforts on releasing the fire burning inside of me. As the seconds ticked by, my lungs began to burn from the lack of oxygen, but I pushed on.

I was anxious to make sure that when I surfaced, the need to light the world around me on fire had abated. Fire ignited beneath the surface causing large bubbles of pressure to burst. My flames were snuffed out on contact once they escaped my hold, but the heat lingered.

When the burn in my chest was too strong to ignore, I rose to the surface.

I sucked in lungfuls of clean air and wiped the droplets clinging to my lashes.

My gaze wandered before finally settling on the concerned face of a black wolf, his head tilted to the side. The water directly around me was still bubbling ever so slightly, near boiling but beginning to wane.

Shame bloomed in my chest, and my anger was redirected at myself. I felt like a failure, a liability to this case. How was I going to find Daniel's murderer if I couldn't keep a lid on my own emotions?

I dragged my sopping wet body out of the Spokane River and climbed back up to the main road. I hadn't realized as I ran that the river was below a small hill, and I struggled as I climbed back out. My soaked boots squelched in the mud as I slipped with each step.

James gave a yip as I approached, his teeth digging into the leather of my coat as he helped drag me up.

When I reached the top ledge, I peeled my leather coat from my shoulders and slung it over my arm, heaving a sigh. That jacket was the first large purchase I had made after receiving my very first paycheck from Mike. I doubted I could save it, but I'd try anyway.

I fingered one of the holes made by James's teeth. "You owe me a new jacket," I told him.

He gave me a noncommittal chuff that almost sounded like a laugh.

I sighed. It was worth a try.

Pushing from the ground, I walked back the way we came. James kept up a steady trot beside me, stopping only to retrieve his clothing along the way.

When the Mustang came within sight, I took in the beautiful car and then my drenched clothing. I heaved another sigh and turned to James. He held his clothing in his mouth, and I looked from him to the car before realization hit.

He couldn't drive. Not in wolf form.

I bent down next to him, ruffling the fur behind his ears for a brief moment before reaching my hand into the pocket of his jeans.

"You won't be needing these," I said, holding his keys up in triumph.

James issued a growl.

I had to laugh.

"Nuh ah ah. Don't be grumpy with me. You're the one that chose to shift. This is on you. I'm just looking out for you and making sure you get home safely."

James growled again as I opened the passenger-side door.

"In you go."

Silver eyes met mine in mutiny, but after a few seconds, he chuffed and jumped inside.

Chapter Ten

Back at my apartment, I quickly changed into dry clothes. Dressed in a warm pair of yoga pants and a black tank, I threw my wet hair into a messy bun before padding out of my room.

James was in human form, shirtless and making tea for the two of us in the kitchen. He handed me a steaming cup. The brew had a floral scent with hints of citrus and was exactly what I needed after the events of today.

James and I sat in comfortable silence, each of us drinking our tea. I was gazing out of the living room window, my thoughts elsewhere, when James took the now-empty cup from my hands.

I looked up from my daze, and watched James walk into the kitchen and place our mugs in the sink. When he came back, rather than taking his seat, he crouched low in front of me. He wrapped his hands around my own. Lines of concern were etched on his face.

"Are you okay?" he asked.

I felt like he was asking me that a lot lately. I nodded before pulling my hands from his grasp.

"Ari, talk to me."

I shook my head. I didn't want to talk. I just wanted to curl into a ball and hide for a while.

James didn't move from his position and leveled me with an encouraging gaze, one filled with understanding and patience.

I cracked.

"I haven't lost control like that in a while. It's just … frustrating," I admitted, my voice hushed.

James nodded in apparent understanding. "Look, we all lose it from time to time."

I shook my head. "You're always in control," I told him, which was true. I'd never seen James go furry unless he wanted to. He was the epitome of self-control and I … well, I wasn't.

"Ari, believe it or not, I lose it from time to time too. I shifted today. It's okay. It doesn't make either of us weak."

I knew he was trying to make me feel better, but my pride had been stung, and his shifting wasn't a loss of control. Not really. He'd realized his wolf needed a release, and he provided it before putting himself in a sticky situation.

My loss of control would have deeply disappointed my father. I refrained from saying that out loud. I didn't need James's pity. "I'm tired," I told him.

He nodded and picked up his shirt that he'd hung across the back of the dining room chair. "I can stay if you want?" He stood by the door with an expression I couldn't quite name.

"It's okay. It's almost three in the morning. You should head home and try to get some sleep."

Was that disappointment that crossed his face?

Before I could think too much about it, he turned and walked out the door, closing it softly behind him.

I stared out my living room window at the early morning traffic and contemplated our progress on finding Daniel's murderer. It took all of two minutes to realize we hadn't made any headway these past two days. There was nothing to go on, and if a lead didn't come in soon, the case would quickly go cold.

Leaving the culprit out there wasn't an option.

I closed the curtains and jumped nearly two feet in the air when the siren on my phone went off. I grabbed my phone from the counter and answered without checking the caller ID. "Naveed," I snapped into the receiver.

"Ms. Naveed, I apologize for the late hour but this is Jackson Harris. I'm with the HPED. I believe we may have some information related to the Daniel Blackmore case."

Yes! I bit back my excited squeal and sat on the arm of my couch. The HPED was the Human and Paranormal Enforcement Division. A call from them, especially at three in the morning, wasn't usually a good sign, but if they had information, then I was happy they were calling. I waited for him to continue.

"There's been another murder with a similar MO. The victim is a shifter with significant blood loss, lacerations across the neck and fang marks on the wrist."

Shit! Another vampire attack? Was it a child again?

Okay, maybe not happy after all.

"I'm on my way," I told him after he rattled off directions. "Have you notified the Pack yet?"

"Not yet. We attempted to through their main contact line but have received no response."

"I'll take care of it," I said. I knew James would answer my call. He likely hadn't even made it home yet.

"And one more thing, Miss Naveed," he said, right before I hung up the phone. "There's a second victim, and this one's not a shifter."

I pinched the bridge of my nose. The way he said it, I knew that whoever the victim was, it was really going to complicate things.

"Who is it?" I asked.

"A female vampire. Found ten yards away, already turning to ash. She must have been extremely old since the desiccation process happened so quickly. But our people have been able to get close up photographs of the body and the damage."

"Cause of death?"

"Visible lacerations, consistent with claw-like patterns. Final cause of death"—he was quiet for a moment—"the heart was ripped from the body."

I thwacked my head against my hand. Could this get any worse?

Chapter Eleven

I arrived at Charley's—a local dive bar—fifteen minutes after the call. The surrounding area was cordoned off with yellow caution tape, and a swarm of people in black uniforms milled around. Some were taking samples from the parking lot, others were writing notes in their notebooks.

The area was devoid of onlookers. Most of Spokane's population knew that when trouble came, it was better to scatter than hang around in case trouble chose to strike again.

It took me several minutes to track down Jackson Harris. Most of the people I asked waved me off, too busy in their own work.

Jackson looked like he'd seen a lot in his career. Dressed in HPED dress blues, he had a weathered expression on his face as he surveyed the scene in front of him. Six feet tall with an average build and sandy blond hair, there was nothing striking about him, and he couldn't be more than forty. He'd easily blended into the crowd, which was probably how he preferred it.

He took me straight to the first body situated right outside the front entrance to the bar. It was a young woman in her late teens, possibly early twenties. She had long blonde hair now matted with blood.

I crouched beside her cold form and gently turned her head left, then right, looking for any clues that may have been missed. Her injuries were similar to Daniel's, but her throat was visibly less mangled than his had been.

Examining her wrists, I pulled out a small retractable ruler from my pocket and measured the distance between the marks. These were about two centimeters wider than the ones found on Daniel.

Strange.

Could there be a copycat killer so quickly? Or maybe whoever murdered Daniel worked with a partner or group.

I visibly shook at the thought. If we were tracking more than one person, it was going to make finding the culprits that much more difficult. Having called James on my way to the scene, I wasn't surprised when I felt him crouch down beside me. He dipped his middle and forefingers in the small puddle of blood that had pooled around the body, before bringing them to his nose and taking a deep breath.

An HPED employee tried to stop him, scolding him for contaminating the crime scene, but one growl and a flash of fang from James sent the man scurrying off. If the victim was a shifter, then the Pack had ruling jurisdiction.

"Shifter?" I asked.

James nodded his head. "Her name was Emma, a werelynx. She lived on the outskirts of the city but came into town from time to time to bar hop with her friends. She was young, twenty-two I think."

"Do you know what she was doing here? If she was with anyone?"

James shook his head. "No, but I'll put in a call to Brock, our head of security. Now that we know who she is, I'll have him question her friends. See if they were out with her this evening. I have a hard time believing her friends would leave the bar without her, had they been with her."

"The HPED unit found the body of a vampire twenty yards that way." Jackson pointed towards the left side of the building. "We'll notify the Coven shortly, but aside from the photographs the MEs took earlier, we have no way of confirming the identity. The body has already turned to ash. The ME and his team are about to sweep the vamp's remains into a containment vessel any minute now."

James swore, a vicious growl following his expletive. Jackson took a step back. His hands held up in a placating gesture.

"How the hell could this happen? Are you sure of the cause of death for both victims? Something isn't adding up here."

"We're sure. I'll have my men send over the full reports as soon as they're wrapped up."

James nodded and then dismissed him. Jackson looked relieved to be able to walk away.

Something was definitely off about this particular murder. The strangest part being that the vampire was in this part of the city. Shifters and vampires had a boundary line of sorts, and neither crossed it. It was an agreement between the two races, and the vampire who had perished was on the wrong side of the proverbial tracks.

On an upside, the shifters couldn't be held responsible for the vampire's death. Once you crossed the line, all bets were off. What the hell had she been doing over here in the first place? She had to have known that her life was forfeit as soon as she crossed over into shifter territory, so why come?

Whatever her reasons, it would have had to be something important to risk herself like this. Clearly, it hadn't panned out.

"If we don't figure this out, and soon, we're going to have a war between the Pack and the Coven. There will be no avoiding it at this rate," James said.

Even though the vampire had entered their territory, he was

right. She was in the wrong, but the Coven would still raise hell for it. We couldn't let things escalate to that point. A war between the vampires and shifters would result in hundreds of casualties, humans included.

I gave James a quick rundown of the differences I'd discovered between Emma's injuries and those found on Daniel, and then gave him some space to go over the scene with his shifter senses in the hope that he would discover something the HPED had missed. The probability was doubtful, now that so many people had passed through the space. It would be near impossible for James to pinpoint anything new, but it was still worth a shot.

Jackson stood next to one of the HPED vehicles a few yards away, talking to two other officers. I'd just taken a step in his direction when movement to my right caught my eye.

I turned to see a shadowy figure move quickly, retreating farther into the alley from where it came.

An onlooker? Maybe they'd seen what had happened.

I pulled my daggers out and cautiously made my way towards the mouth of the alley, keeping my eyes on the now still, shadowed form. I didn't make it a habit of threatening innocent bystanders, but I wasn't going to walk in unarmed either. "Show yourself!" I called out, as I got closer.

Surprisingly, he did.

A shock of recognition thrummed through me as I came face to face with my new neighbor. Brows furrowed, I considered what his involvement might be as I studied him.

Inarus was wearing dark denim jeans and a long sleeved black thermal shirt. The flickering streetlights shone on something small and metallic in his hands.

I stiffened. "What are you doing here?"

He looked over my shoulder to the alley entrance as if debating what to say before returning his gaze to mine. "I'm watching over you," he said, shrugging.

Great. I had a crazy stalker. Just what every girl needed.

"I don't need anyone to watch over me, and I don't know you. How about you cut the crap and tell me why you're really here?"

As his blue-grey eyes met mine, I felt the temperature rise along with my irritation. The heat was still within my range of control, so I allowed myself to sink into it as the waves rolled over my neck and shoulders.

"I can see the fire within you. Even now when it's buried deep below the surface, your eyes have that orange glow."

Mouth hanging open and eyes growing wide, I took an involuntary step back. How did he know? Shock coursed through me, quickly replaced by a jolt of fear at the implications. My powers, in the wrong hands, could have catastrophic consequences, and somehow this stranger knew about them. How? Mike and James were the only people I trusted with my secret.

A million thoughts ran through my mind. Had Inarus seen me use my pyrokinetic abilities somehow? If so, where? When? How did I miss him?

No. No. No.

"You're wondering how I know, right? If I stumbled upon you one day when you were reckless."

I didn't bother answering, too dumbfounded to even know what to say.

"You weren't reckless, Aria."

I shook my head. I didn't remember ever giving him my name.

Inarus took two steps closer. "But I know you're a psyker, because I am, too." Without any more explanation, he opened his palm and showed me three small metal spheres. I raised my daggers. I didn't know what he was planning, but I was confident in my abilities. I could take him.

Before I could blink, all three floated in the air a few inches above his right palm. Rapidly they started spinning clockwise, and my gaze was transfixed on their movement.

All too quickly, he released whatever hold he had on the spheres and snapped his hand closed, hiding them within as he shoved his hand in his jean pocket.

"You're not like me," was the first thought that tumbled out of my mouth. Inwardly, I cursed my stupidity. Telling him he wasn't like me only confirmed I wasn't human.

Way to go, Aria.

"No, not exactly. You're a pyrokinetic. I'm a telekinetic. Our abilities are different in how they work and what we can do with them, but we're both psykers."

"Awesome. I'm happy for you. Now, if you don't mind—"

James called out my name in the distance.

I threw a glance over my shoulder. "I need to get back," I told him, slowly backing away from the alley like he was a predator getting ready to spring.

"Go ahead, run away. I'll catch up to you later." His words held an underlying threat that had my blood running cold.

"I'm not running," I snapped.

"Sure you're not."

I glared at him. Maybe I was running, but what was I supposed to do? A sexy stranger, who happened to be my new neighbor, just told me he had psychic powers. I didn't know who he was or what organization he belonged to, but whatever it was, it couldn't be good.

"Look, I'm not running. But I don't want any part of whatever it is you're involved in."

"You make it sound nefarious. I'm a friend. You can relax. When you're up for it, why don't we grab coffee sometime? We can talk."

"Sure." I waved him off. "Sometime." I needed to get farther away from him, not closer. There was no way in hell I'd be meeting him anywhere in the foreseeable future. I made a hasty retreat, leaving Inarus in the darkened alley. The more steps I took, the more control I got over my racing heartbeat.

I chanced a look over my shoulder, but he was gone.

Fuck me. This couldn't be good.

"Anything?" I asked James as I came closer. James shook his head in irritation, his entire focus on the scene before him. I wasn't surprised he'd missed my brief absence. When he was on a hunt, he was wholly focused.

"No, the entire area is coated in a fine layer of wolfsbane. I can't smell anything."

I was considering telling him about my strange encounter with my neighbor when his words sunk in.

"Wolfsbane?" I asked, needing the confirmation.

James nodded again.

"Why would there be wolfsbane here?" Wolfsbane wasn't easy to come by, so whoever had used it knew shifters would be on scene and had had enough forethought to come prepared. If I needed any additional confirmation, this was it.

Tonight's events hadn't been an accident.

"Your guess is as good as mine, but someone added it and made sure to cover not only the bodies but a perimeter extending thirty feet in each direction. This is smelling more and more like a setup, Ari." His tone was grim.

My mind raced over everything I knew. Daniel Blackmore had gone missing a little over two weeks ago. We'd found his mutilated body dumped not far from the invisible border separating Pack and Coven territories. While Emma's death appeared similar—twin fang marks on the wrist, slit throat—that was where the similarities ended. Fangs don't widen in a vamp's mouth, so Emma's fang marks were clearly made by a different vampire. And, unlike Daniel, she had been left otherwise unblemished. No broken bones or ripped-open flesh.

We didn't have much on our third victim aside from being a

female vampire, name and age unknown. And cause of death was consistent with an animal or shifter attack.

That final thought gave me pause.

"Hey, James—"

"What?" He didn't bother to look up as he crouched down and poked through the vampire ashes with a pencil.

"Could Emma maintain a between form?" I wasn't an expert on shifters by any means, but I did know that if a shifter died in animal form, they didn't revert back to human, they remained animals. If a shifter died while in their between form though, they did revert back to human. If Emma couldn't maintain a between form, then it was doubtful that she'd been able to cause our other victim's injuries.

James shook his head. "No, she was too young to have acquired the skill. She could only shift to her full beast."

"Is there a way for you to tell if Emma had gone, you know, furry or not? And whether she shifted back before her death?"

James quirked a brow. "What are you thinking, Ari?"

I began pacing in the street, letting my thoughts tumble out of my mouth. "I'm thinking this was all a set-up. That maybe Emma and whoever our unknown vamp is over there didn't actually have any sort of altercation. Jackson showed me the photos of the body before it turned to ash. It has claw marks without a doubt, and the heart had been ripped from the victim's chest, but what if Emma wasn't the one that did it? What if our unknown vamp didn't kill Emma either?"

James's eyes lit up, clearly following my train of thought.

"Don't you see?" I continued. "Why else would someone sprinkle the area with wolfsbane? Someone is trying to cover their tracks, but this"—I waved my arms in the direction of the two bodies. "This screams set-up, and if Emma can't maintain a between form, how did she kill our vampire victim and then die in human form?"

James was nodding his head, and the gears in my mind were

spinning. The sound of vehicle motors starting up caught my attention, and James and I watched the HPED begin moving out.

What the hell?

I jogged over to Jackson as he climbed into his black SUV. "What's going on?" I asked him.

"We've been called off. This isn't a human problem, so we're pulling out," he said.

You have got to be kidding me. "What about the bodies?" I asked, indicating the scene. Jackson shrugged his shoulders.

"Half the vamp is already gone, the rest will float away in the breeze by morning and your friend there—" he said, indicating James, "—will take care of the shifter girl."

I gritted my teeth. This was so like the HPED. They'd come to scope things out, but if it wasn't a quick and easy job, they bailed and moved on.

This was why crime was so high in our city. Why things had yet to stabilize after the Awakening.

Stomping back to James, I filled him in. On a curse filled with disgust, he pulled out his cell and dialed a number. I assumed he was calling the Pack to have Emma's body picked up.

Still frustrated over the situation, I went and pulled my HAZMAT kit out of the trunk of my Civic. The four-by-three-foot steel case housed virtually everything needed to collect evidence. In addition to the case, I pulled out a gallon-sized glass container and a battery-operated mini vac. You could never be too prepared. I lugged the items over to the vampire remains, opened my case, then unscrewed the lid on the glass jar.

"What are you doing?" James asked over my shoulder, having ended his call.

"Cleaning up." I pulled on a pair of rubber gloves.

He eyed my mini vac skeptically. It was probably in poor taste to vacuum up the dead, but well, it isn't like I had many options and frankly, a vacuum was going to be more effective than a broom and dustpan.

"What did the Pack say?" I asked. I pulled several chemical light sticks from my case and cracked them until they offered a faint glow. I placed one inside of the glass jar and placed the other two near the pile of ash-coated remains. The glow sticks did little to illuminate the space, forcing me to rely on the dim streetlights, but what they did do was cast the vampire remains in a blue glow separating them from typical dirt and debris, so nothing was missed.

"Devin and Brock are five minutes out. They'll pick up Emma's body while I go report to Declan."

I nodded my head as I used a small wooden stick to poke around at the remains. James made a coughing noise mixed with a gag, and I turned around to look at him, a wry grin on my face.

"You doing okay there, buddy?" I mocked.

"That's disgusting." James wrinkled his face and took a few steps back.

"You were just poking it a few minutes ago," I reminded him.

"That was different. I wasn't paying attention to the gunk buried beneath, and I wasn't unburying that retched smell."

"Suck it up, buttercup. It's all part of the job." I turned back to the task at hand.

Small particles of the vampire's body were hovering eerily in the air like dust motes, having risen from my poking around. I pulled out several pieces of bone too large for my vacuum to suck up and tossed them into the glass container. The fact that large remnants remained meant the vampire was young, relatively speaking. No more than fifty undead years.

My concentration was suddenly broken by the roar of an approaching car. James and I looked toward the sound to see a black Hummer fitted out like a tank with guardrails and roll bars. It stopped a few yards from the crime site, and two men climbed out.

The driver wore form-fitting jeans that hugged his thighs and a navy blue T-shirt that showed off his massive bulk and broad shoulders. Wearing a grim expression, he made his way towards us. If I had to guess, he looked to be in his mid-thirties.

The passenger was younger, maybe mid-twenties, with boyish features, a full mouth, and long limbs that had yet to fill out entirely.

The two men approached on silent feet. James inclined his head towards both men, offering a small greeting before leading them to Emma's body while I continued my work with the vamp's.

I watched the three men from the corner of my eye as they lifted Emma and placed her gently into a blue body bag before setting her in the rear of the Hummer.

The younger of the two newcomers poured a white fluid where the body had been that sizzled upon contact. White bubbles formed as it destroyed any part of the blood or bodily fluids that may have remained.

The Lyc-V virus was highly contagious. Unlike in the stories, it wasn't a shifter bite that could turn a human. It was blood-to-blood contamination. It was one of many reasons that humans feared shifters, and why several of the HPED members had been avoiding the body. No one wanted to accidentally get infected.

But every shifter I'd ever met was always extremely conscious of their ability to infect non-shifters and most carried at least a small measure of LVP with them at all times. LVP was a liquid substance that killed the virus outside of the host. Lycanthropy had an hour window of infection. Once the blood expired, the virus died, but since James wasn't sticking around, the Pack was making sure no one stumbled by while it was still active.

With his task complete, the driver went back to his Hummer and headed out as James walked back toward me.

"Brock's going to ride back with me since I'm going back to the Compound. How much longer will you be?" he asked.

"A while," I told him. "You two go ahead. I'll be fine."

James looked conflicted for a moment.

"Go," I told him again, waving him away, "I'm a big girl. I can take care of myself."

He sighed. "Fine, but call me when you head out okay?"

"Yes, Mom," I said with a snicker.

"Haha. Very funny."

I watched as James and Brock went towards the Mustang, and after fishing the last bit of bone from the pile, pulled my mini vac out and began vacuuming up the ashy remains.

The sound of the vacuum drowned out the city as I hummed along to a silent tune, making sure to catch all of the particles. I had to empty the vacuum canister into the glass jar three times before I finally had it all. It wasn't my job to act as Hazmat clean up. The HPED should have taken care of that. Lazy jerks. But I didn't like the idea of anyone wandering upon a pile of dead vamp. So, here I was. Playing housekeeper to the city.

James was long gone by now. The streets were quiet. The area now vacant in the early morning hours. I took a quick peek at my watch. It was only three hours till sunrise, and a yawn reminded me that I'd barely gotten any sleep.

I pulled out a small bottle of bleach and poured it over the concrete where the body had once been, making sure to coat the area evenly and cover a slightly larger perimeter to be on the safe side. Vampirism wasn't contagious the way lycanthropy was. You did, in fact, have to be bitten, multiple times actually, but dead-body particles were still dead-body particles. Who knew what heeby jeebies you could contract?

As I screwed the cap back onto the bleach bottle, the hairs on the back of my neck rose. I tossed my supplies back into the metal case and allowed instinct to guide me.

I wasn't alone.

Without being too obvious, I scanned my surroundings as I

busied myself with the latch on the case. Everything back in its place, I quickly shut it, grabbed my vacuum, and hauled it all back to my little Civic, all the while keeping my eyes peeled for trouble.

I trusted my instincts, and they were screaming at me to get the hell out of here. Now. I just needed to make it to my car. My Honda wasn't anything spectacular on the outside, but I'd customized the thing to survive almost any kind of assault. The windows were quarter-inch-thick bulletproof glass, and the frame had been reinforced, encased in high mobility armor, even the underside, leaving it virtually indestructible.

My little Civic could take on a tank, and while the tank would probably win, my car would put up one hell of a fight. You couldn't get a tougher car. Whoever or whatever was stalking me through the night wouldn't get the chance to take a shot at me once I was safely inside.

Easier said than done.

Adrenaline coursed through me, urging me to run. I quickened my pace. The feeling of being exposed increased tenfold, and I nearly dropped the metal case in my rush to get to my car. I tried to shake off the feeling of unease. Was this just morning jitters? I couldn't see anyone. Let alone hear anything but still …

I finally made it to my car and quickly unlocked the trunk, tossing the case and vacuum in before jogging to the driver side door. My hand was on the door handle, a wave of relief washing over me. I'd made it.

Crack!

Something slammed into the back of my head, and a bright burst of pain shot through me. My skull connected with the top of my car, and my vision blurred. Fuck.

Fight or flight took hold, and dammit, I was a fighter.

I struggled to hold myself upright as the world spun around me. I leaned against the Civic, trying to regain my balance when another blow to my head had me stumbling backward, away from the safety of my vehicle.

Shit. "Pull it together," I growled to myself.

I tried to pull fire and target my attacker, but the pain in my head wouldn't allow me to focus. The air whooshed out of my lungs as my attacker landed a kick to my ribs. A sharp stab of pain and the distinct sound of bone breaking was a sure sign at least one of my ribs had cracked. I clutched my stomach, gasping for breath. Breathing was becoming more and more difficult.

"What do you want?" I gasped. Multiple silhouettes of my attacker danced in front me, but I couldn't zero in on him. I put my hand over my left eye and tried to pull the three swimming figures into one.

Gotcha.

I threw a punch, connected with a jaw, heard my attacker curse, and then was thrown to the pavement.

"Ow!" I complained. "Look, if you're going to be a big enough dick to attack an unsuspecting woman, the least you could do is give me a minute to catch my breath."

I struggled to sit up and heard a distinctly male laugh. The soft sound of his footsteps against asphalt grew louder as he came closer to my prone form.

I took several labored breaths and clutched my ribcage. Everything hurt.

My head felt as if a thousand little people were hammering away inside. I rolled to my side clawing at the asphalt in an attempt to stay conscious. My attacker crouched in front of me. Grabbing my chin with cold fingers, he tilted my head upward. Three sets of bright crimson eyes glowing with menace slowly focused into one and met my gaze.

He smiled, his fangs evident now that he was close up. Vampire. That wasn't good. Why was a vampire attacking me? What the hell had I done to him?

Confusion rolled through me. Did he think I was the one

responsible for killing the vamp? I had been vacuuming up her remains. I could see how someone could get the wrong idea.

"Look, buddy—"

"Such a shame." His rich, cultured voice was like velvet along my senses.

I felt the compulsion—that mind domination only vampires possessed—trying to take over. I struggled against the lulling effect of his deep voice. He yanked my head to the side, exposing the sensitive skin of my neck. I struggled against his iron grip, trying to reach for my daggers, but it was no use.

"I didn't kill her, you asshole!"

I was defenseless from the angle he held my head. His warm breath caressed my neck, making me shiver. He inhaled deeply and lowered his mouth.

"Shhh … don't fight it," he whispered. My muscles relaxed against what little control I had left, as my mind panicked.

Come on, Aria. You are not going to become a vampire snack. This is not how you're going to go out. Dammit.

He ran his tongue along the column of my neck, the sensation causing my stomach to revolt. The scrape of his fangs on my sensitive flesh jolted me from his thrall, and I struggled against his hold. My temperature rose and my fire finally surfaced. Thank God!

But not fast enough. The vampire chuckled under his breath, and just as flames licked my skin in a gentle caress, my attacker was thrown off of me.

As I quickly turned my head to see what had happened, a sharp pain shot into my skull. I gasped. Taking a deep breath, I forced myself to slow down and turned my head slower. A thin veil of flames clouded my vision, but only for a moment.

The vampire was slumped against a nearby brick building. A wound on the side of his skull bled profusely, and he sported a gaping hole in his chest. His eyes had dimmed to a dull red. The glow no longer evident.

Inarus stood before him like an avenging angel, holding a pulsing red mass of flesh in his outstretched hand.

Oh, my God, it was a heart. He'd ripped out his heart! I tried to get my head around that. He had literally ripped the vampire's heart from his body. How the hell had he done that?

Struggling into a sitting position, I cradled my stomach. The pain was hitting me full force now as the adrenaline dissipated. I moaned, and my head began to swim. I wavered where I sat.

The upside was, if I collapsed, the fall wouldn't be all that far. The downside was that I didn't know this guy. Nor did I trust him. If I passed out now, who knew what would happen to me?

Inarus turned at the sound of my pained groan. His eyes blazed a bright blue, and he wore a grim expression. Looking down, his expression changed to one of surprise when he realized he was still clutching the vampire's heart. He dropped it like it was nothing more than a piece of trash, made his way to where I was sitting, and crouched down.

I flinched when he reached out for me.

"Aria, call your fire back." His words were an order. His eyes locked on mine.

Defiance rose up in side me. *Hell no!* My fire was the only thing keeping me safe. If I called that back, he could … well he could do a lot of things, and none of the possibilities running through my mind were friendly.

"You're hurt. I just want to check you out."

I laughed, but it came out more like a pained wheeze. "I'm good. Your assistance won't be necessary." I tried to stand and made it all of two inches from the ground before collapsing.

Inarus placed his palms on either side of my face, the one part of my body currently fire free. His skin felt cool compared to my overheated flesh, and I leaned into his hold slightly, enjoying the comfort his touch brought.

"Let me help you," he implored me.

I tried to speak, but a flash of pain consumed me. I bit back the tears threatening to form in the corners of my eyes.

"I won't hurt you. You have my word." His eyes were earnest, and something inside of me eased. I needed help. I knew that. And I didn't have a lot of options here.

Muttering a curse, I slowly called in my fire. If he wanted to kill me, he could have already. I was going to just have to take my chances.

With my flames gone, he carefully folded me into his arms. The movement made my body scream in protest. I gasped audibly, barely containing a sob of agony.

I bit my cheek until I tasted blood, trying to hold it. Just breathe. You've been through worse. This is nothing. Keep it together. I repeated the mantra over and over in my head.

"I know. I'm so sorry, Aria," he whispered the words into my hair as he rose to his full height, my body nestled in his strong arms. "This is going to hurt. I'll go as slow as possible but …" He trailed off.

I nodded and closed my eyes, allowing him to carry me over to my Civic. He opened the door carefully and gently helped me inside before going around and climbing into the driver's seat.

"Keys?" he asked.

I pulled my keys from my pocket and handed them to him with shaking fingers. When his hand brushed mine, I looked up, our gazes colliding.

His lips pursed. He looked angry, but I knew his anger wasn't directed at me. That was good.

Without a word, he started the ignition and pulled out of the parking lot. I didn't get the chance to ask where he was taking me before unconsciousness tugged at me, and I fell into its dark embrace.

Chapter Twelve

I woke up to the feel of a warm, damp cloth running along my abdomen. On a pain-filled moan, I opened my eyes to find Inarus leaning over my prone form, a washcloth in his hand.

His eyes met mine as he gently stroked the cloth over me, wiping away the dirt and grime from this evening's events. Or more accurately, this morning's.

When I didn't object to his attentions, he looked away. I watched him concentrate on my body, his eyes never wavering from his task. He seemed to pay special attention to the blade tattooed above my right hip as he stroked carefully over my bruised flesh. A question was evident in his stare, but he never voiced it.

That was good, because I didn't plan on answering. We all had secrets. The magical properties behind my dagger tattoo was one of mine.

I noticed that my arms were already clean, and I could see some blood and discolored skin through the holes in my pants, but that could all wait. He couldn't do anything about my legs without taking off my pants. That wasn't happening.

When Inarus finished cleaning my abdomen and the exposed

skin above my breasts, he dropped the cloth in a small water-filled bowl.

His gaze assessed me, and I began to fidget under his scrutiny.

"I need to press on your stomach to see how much damage was done. This may hurt a bit," he told me.

I nodded and braced myself.

He gently pushed, poked, and prodded my stomach. At first, the pain was bearable, but as his fingers climbed higher, I was no longer able to stay quiet. I gasped and groaned when he pushed down once more, his fingers digging into my flesh. Tears leaked from my eyes, and I grew furious with myself for letting them out.

"You have a cracked rib," he told me. "Most likely a concussion as well, judging from the size of the bruise blooming on your forehead."

I reached up and touched my head. The skin was tender, and a knot was forming above my right eye. Wasn't that just peachy.

I ran my fingers gently over my skull, feeling several more. I definitely had a concussion. My vision was blurred, and I was dazed even while lying back.

Inarus reached for the cloth once again and wrung out the excess blood-stained water before carefully sweeping it across my cheek. The water stung the minor cuts and scrapes on my face, but I held still as he wiped away the dried flakes of blood.

I couldn't help but wince at the sting of what was surely a split lip. Inarus's eyes flew to my face. He held the cloth motionless against my lips, his gaze boring into mine. I fought the urge to fidget against the sudden rush of attraction I was feeling. An attraction that was apparently not reciprocated.

If my proximity didn't affect him, then I wouldn't allow his to affect me.

Seriously, Ari. You need to get a hold on your libido. First James and now him? Well, I guess technically Inarus came first, but still. Not cool.

Completing his task with cool detachment, he placed the rag in the bowl again and set it aside. Then he reached for my boots and unlaced them with smooth efficiency. Gently pulling them off, he set them on the floor beside the bed. A bed that most certainly did not belong to me. "Are you okay?" His voice had warmed just a fraction.

"I'm fine. Thank you," I mumbled around my swollen lip.

He raised a brow as he considered my response. We both knew I was far from fine. A cracked rib, a concussion, and several cuts and bruises didn't equal fine. But after a moment of silence, he nodded.

"Where am I?" I asked.

Inarus offered a small smile that made my heart give a pathetic flutter. Gah, what was wrong with me? Maybe I'd experienced more severe head trauma than I'd thought.

Yeah. That sounded right. I'd blame this on the head injury.

"You're in my apartment. I wasn't sure how you'd feel about a hospital, so this was the next best thing."

I thanked my lucky stars that he hadn't taken me to any of the hack medical facilities that the city called hospitals. Testing centers were more like it. They didn't truly help the sick or the injured. No. The doctors were more like mad scientists, focusing on their experiments, especially on anyone showing signs of being more than human.

I'd never actually tested my own blood, but I had a feeling my DNA was a tad bit different from your average Homo sapiens, and I wasn't one for taking unnecessary risks.

Well, usually.

Okay, I often took unnecessary risks. But I wasn't an idiot.

"Thank you," I told him, and I genuinely meant it. A shiver ran through me just thinking about what would have happened had he taken me to River Park Hospital or worse, Holy Trinity

Hospital. I wouldn't take a dog there if it were dying. Allowing the animal to die would probably be the more humane choice.

"No problem. Besides, you owe me a cup of coffee. Remember?" He grinned wide and handed me a cup of steaming coffee that I hadn't noticed earlier.

I took the warm cup gratefully and inhaled the delicious aroma, ignoring the protest from my cracked rib.

Coffee could fix this. Coffee could fix anything. I smiled at him in thanks and took a sip before realizing my mouth didn't want to cooperate. Damn split lip.

Inarus handed me a straw, a grin on his face, and I closed my eyes in relief as I took my first sip. The heady flavor exploded on my taste buds. I groaned in pleasure and sank back into the pillows. I didn't care if I was drinking it like a grandma in a nursing home. Hell, I'd drink it out of a sippy cup if I had to.

He chuckled, but I didn't bother opening my eyes. Instead, I took another sip, allowing the liquid to flow through me as if it were an IV hooked directly to my veins. Oh, I needed this.

"I take it you like coffee?" Inarus asked.

I opened one eye, gave him an annoyed look, then closed it once more and took another drink. "There is no such thing as just liking coffee," I told him between sips. "I love coffee more than a vamp loves blood. It's essential to my survival."

He chuckled. "I need to wrap your ribs." He reached for a stack of bandages, and I pulled myself forward, setting the coffee down on the nightstand. I lifted the hem of my shirt to expose my rib cage.

Inarus deftly wrapped the bandage around my body, and I sucked in a breath every time his hand brushed against my tender flesh. The pain of sitting up was excruciating, but I bit my cheek and kept quiet. Having the bandage in place surprisingly took some of the edge off.

He helped me lean back against the pillows, and I reached for my coffee once more. I closed my eyes and sipped at the straw only to realize it was empty.

Dammit.

"Here, this will do more for you than the coffee will." Inarus placed three white pills in the palm of my hand.

"What are they?" I asked. I eyed the pills skeptically. He handed me a small bottle, and I turned it over in my free hand to read the label. Acetaminophen with codeine.

Holy hell. How did he manage to get his hands on pain pills? Without another thought, I tossed back the pills and swallowed them down.

The Awakening had been the end of most big box pharmaceutical companies—those that had been primarily government-funded at least—so any type of medication was a rare find and likely cost a fortune. Instead of having a few pills stashed away in case of an emergency like most people did, he had a whole freaking bottle.

"Get some sleep," he told me, and took the pill bottle back. "I'll make sure to check in on you."

I already felt the effects of the medication. Rather than an ache in my head, I felt light, airy, almost as if I were floating out of my body. I gave Inarus a goofy grin.

"I need to go home," I announced, hefting myself away from the pillows I was leaning against, and swinging my legs over the side of the bed.

Clenching my teeth to hold the gasp of pain inside, I closed my eyes, giving myself a moment to catch my breath and work through the pain. Just a few more minutes, and the painkiller would kick in all the way. Then I'd be good to go.

"Aria, you're not going anywhere. You're hurt. The concussion alone is reason enough that you shouldn't be by yourself."

That was all fine and dandy, but that didn't mean I would stay.

Inarus was my new sexy, nosey, and totally unknown

neighbor. I'd be an idiot if I stayed with him. If I could just make it out of the bed and down the hallway, I could collapse into my own bed. I'd be fine.

While I was grateful to Inarus for helping me, he was a stranger. That was strike one. He was also a psyker. Strike two. Therefore, due to reason one and reason two, I couldn't trust him. Strike three. You're out.

I needed the comfort of my own bed and time alone to wrap my head around the events of tonight and figure out why the hell I'd been attacked in the first place. By a vampire. In shifter territory.

Unfortunately, I couldn't question my attacker because he was dead.

I stared at Inarus with a mutinous expression. He couldn't make me stay here. If the hardening of his features was any indication though, he still planned to try.

"You're staying," he gritted out through clenched teeth.

"No. I'm. Not," I enunciated, making sure he heard me clearly.

I stood and watched through narrowed eyes as Inarus took a few steps back. My limbs shook, and my head swam with the effort to stay conscious. Don't pass out. Don't pass out. All I had to do was make it to my apartment. The doorway leading to freedom was only steps away. "I can do this," I told myself. I breathed through my mouth and waited for my vision to clear.

Inarus stood to the side, arms folded across his chest. There would be no help from him.

I took a tentative step, and the world tilted. A bare second before I landed on the carpeted floor, he was there to catch me. He eased me into his arms and rose, cradling me tenderly against his chest.

"Put me down." The sound of my own voice caused me to cringe inside. It was pathetic and whiny even to my own ears.

He didn't react other than to lay me back down on the bed's

cool sheets. He sat by my side and the mattress sank under his weight?

"You're staying," he reiterated.

I glared daggers at him.

"You can't make me," I bit out.

"You're right, but I can wait you out. One of the pills I gave you may have been a sedative," he admitted, a sly smile curving his lips.

What? The bastard drugged me? See! I knew I couldn't trust him. Where the hell did he …

The thought drifted away as the room began to darken. "Stop messing with the lights." The pull of the sedative was strong. My eyes drifted closed, and my body sank deeper into the warmth and comfort of the bed.

"Get some rest." His voice seemed to come from another room. A hand gently touched my cheek and slid along my neck before disappearing.

Wait! I wanted to shout.

"I'll be here when you wake."

Chapter Thirteen

I woke to a pounding in my head and an insistent buzzing noise. It took me a moment to realize that the two were not related.

Bzzp.

Bzzp.

Bzzp.

Stupid phone. Where had I put that thing?

Finding it buried in the sheets, I answer with a mumbled, "Hello." Not bothering to check caller ID.

"Aria, where the hell are you?" was the angry response I received.

"Ouch! No need to yell." My brain felt like a bowl of oatmeal. "I'm in bed. Where are you?"

"I'm at your apartment. It's empty. So, I'll ask again, where the hell are you? You were supposed to call me last night. Do you have any idea how worried I've been?"

I looked up at the sound of footsteps.

"Hey, you're up." Inarus stood in the doorway. "How are you feeling?"

I held up a finger, indicating that I needed a minute.

"Who's that with you?" James growled into the phone.

"Do you want anything for breakfast?" Inarus grinned like the cat that ate the canary. So much for taking the hint.

"Who the hell is that, Aria?!"

Oh dear, James just called me Aria instead of Ari. He. Was. Pissed. And now he was yelling. I held my phone away from my ear, hoping to still make out what he was saying without popping an eardrum.

I shook my head in response to Inarus's question and, finally taking the cue, he silently retreated back to where he came from.

"Aria, tell me what the hell is going on? Are you with some guy right now?"

My frustration was growing by the second. Who the hell did he think he was, my keeper? "Look, not that it's any of your business," I bit out. "But I'm at a friend's. I'll call you later." I snapped my cell phone shut, cutting off any response he may have had, and rested my head back on my pillow. I probably shouldn't have yelled at him. He was only concerned. But good grief, he was acting jealous!

Heaving a sigh, I looked around the room, noticing details I had been too out of it to notice before. Similar in size to my own bedroom, the walls were painted a soft grey, giving the space a surprisingly warm, cozy feel. I glanced down at the blue sheets, the blue and brown plaid bedspread, and wondered if Inarus had chosen them to go with the grey walls.

The only other item in the room, besides the bed, was the nightstand and a small desk nestled in the corner, small stacks of paper neatly arranged on top.

Unlike my mess of a room, the floor was empty of clothes, shoes, and other belongings. Going off of first impressions, I'd say Inarus was a neat freak. But then, I was somewhat of a slob, so my opinion might be considered questionable.

Throwing my legs over the side of the bed, I stood up and

released a breath of relief that the dizziness was gone, but cringed over the stiffness in my muscles and joints.

Point one for Aria. Clenching my teeth against the ache in my ribs, I padded to the doorway. A heavenly smell came from the hall, and I allowed my nose to lead the way.

The heavenly smell turned out to be bacon and maple syrup. Mmmm.

Sore muscles be damned, I couldn't resist getting closer and came to stand beside Inarus at the stove. He transferred bacon from a frying pan to an empty plate situated beside another, larger plate stacked with buttery pancakes. My mouth watered. Mmmm that looked good.

"How are you feeling?" He gave me a quick once-over.

"Better. Thanks." My stomach rumbled. I was feeling a lot better than I should after the injuries I'd sustained the previous night, and I was starving.

He nodded and grabbed the pancakes. He brought them over to the dining room table already set with two round plates, utensils, and two glasses of orange juice.

Indicating the chair closest to me he placed the food on the table and pulled out my chair. Moving closer, I allowed him to help me into my seat before he took his own.

When my stomach rumbled again, I chanced a look in his direction and caught him staring with a wide grin on his face. "What?" I asked.

"Nothing," he responded. "Just thought you didn't want anything."

"Yeah, well, I guess I changed my mind. Woman's prerogative and all that jazz."

He flashed me another grin before digging into his food, and not long after, I followed suit. We ate in comfortable silence, and I savored every bite. The pancakes were light and fluffy, like heaven coated in syrup and sugar.

I'd never been a fan of them before, but I was officially converted.

When my stack was gone, I frowned at my empty plate until I remembered the bacon. I dove into that, swiping each piece in the remaining syrupy goodness. I hadn't even noticed that Inarus was gone until he walked back into the kitchen holding a pile of clothing.

"They're probably too big, but they should do. I figured you'd want to get cleaned up."

"That'd be great. Thanks," I said. I hadn't even noticed my bloodstained clothing or the fact that it was ripped in several places, exposing more flesh than I'd have liked. Now that he'd brought it to my attention, I felt exposed.

Inarus pointed me in the direction of the bathroom, and off I went. I wasn't worried about being presentable. That ship had already sailed. But I'd settle for clean and covered.

Minutes later I was relaxing under the warm spray when a loud banging had me jumping out of the enclosure. I swiped one of my daggers from the bathroom counter and made a dead run for the front of the apartment, ignoring the throbbing in my ribs as adrenaline surged.

I raced across the carpeted floors, hearing bodies crash and glass shatter in the room ahead of me. I called my fire, ready to burn whoever our attacker was, when I skidded to a halt in the open doorway leading to the living room.

Inarus and James were rolling across the floor. The furniture was in shambles all around them.

"What the hell is going on?" I shouted over their grunts and curses.

At the sound of my voice, they stopped and looked up at me like little boys caught fighting. The anger emanating from them both dissipated, and they stared at me, mouths open in dumbfounded shock.

What the hell?

It only took me a second to realize I was stark naked and dripping wet.

Shit!

In my haste, I'd run out of the bathroom without even a towel to hide my nudity. I gave a shriek and ran back into the safety of the hallway. Yanking open a random door, I sighed with relief that it happened to be a closet and grabbed the large sweatshirt inside and threw it on.

I took a deep breath and strolled back into the living room, chin held high, ignoring the fact that I was still very wet and very naked under Inarus's hoodie. Thankfully, it came down to my knees. I wasn't shy by any means, but I wasn't the type to prance around naked either.

"Do either of you want to explain what the hell is going on?" I filled my voice with authority and irritation and acted as if I hadn't just been parading my goods in front of them both.

James and Inarus were exactly as I'd left them, locked in one another's grip on the floor as if they'd been frozen in place.

At my question they released one another. But both of their expressions said they weren't finished.

"Well?" I asked again, tapping my foot.

"What do you mean, 'well,' Aria? I think you have some explaining to do," James countered. Tiny ripples broke out along his skin. He was losing it, and his wolf wanted out. I needed to defuse the situation and do it fast or I'd have a very pissed off wolf on the loose.

"I already told you," I bit out.

He scoffed. "Oh, really? 'At a friends'?' I didn't realize you ran around naked at all your friends' houses. Or maybe just your other friends."

Yep, definitely jealous. Great.

I threw my hands in the air then winced at the sharp stab of pain that spread through my chest. Stupid ribs were still healing. *Urgh! Come on psyker super healing. Time to kick into overdrive before these knuckleheads kill one another.*

James was being ridiculous, and I was going to tell him exactly that. But before I could open my mouth, Inarus cut in.

"Look at her," he pointed at me. "Seriously, look at her. The split lip, the bruising on her cheek and temple. What do you really think is going on here? You can even see the bruises and cuts on her legs."

That stopped James for a moment, and his angry gaze roved over my body. It took him only a second or two to realize that I had sustained injuries and that he was acting like a complete ass. Between one breath and the next, he was in front of me. Cupping my cheeks in his calloused palms as he examined my injuries up close. When he released me, he bit out a foul curse before sweeping me into his arms and burying his nose in my neck.

"I'm so sorry," he whispered into my hair. "I should have been there. I shouldn't have left you alone."

I bit my lip to hold in a cry of pain. He was squeezing too hard, but I knew he needed this. Knew his wolf needed the contact to calm down. So I waited until he was ready to let me go. Several minutes passed before he finally pulled back, but he kept his hands on my waist. "What happened?"

I shook my head, my eyes suddenly misting. God, this was frustrating. I wasn't used to someone worrying over me, and knowing that James cared, that he was concerned for my well-being, put a crack in the thick brick wall I had meticulously built over the years.

"I'm fine." I pulled away and looked down at my bare feet.

James growled, a thick rumbling sound that vibrated within his chest. "Sit down and tell me everything."

I shook my head and gave him a smile. He had such a temper.

James narrowed his eyes. A silent demand.

Heaving a sigh, I conceded and sat beside him on the couch. Some battles weren't worth the fight.

I recounted every detail about the attack that I could

remember. When I was finished, James looked like he was ready to commit murder.

"Christ, Ari. I never should have you left alone." James uttered a few more choice words and then looked over at Inarus and did the chin lift—man code for thanks, dude.

I rolled my eyes when Inarus returned the gesture. Men were idiots.

With the playback complete and proper introductions made between the two knuckleheads, I headed back down the hall to finish rinsing the shampoo from my hair and throw on more appropriate clothes.

I came back out in an oversized T-shirt knotted with a hair tie and a pair of grey sweats that I rolled at the waist so they didn't drag. Inarus and James were both seated at the dining room table, eyes locked in a battle of wills.

Well, this was going to be fun.

Inarus looked at ease, his small metallic spheres hovering in a circular motion in the palm of his right hand. But the stiff set of his shoulders said otherwise.

He clearly didn't mind if anyone knew his secrets.

James also gave off a false sense of relaxation. He was leaning back in his chair, the front legs lifted slightly off the ground as he balanced the chair with one foot. He had his arm hooked over the top of the chair, and while his posture was relaxed, the look he was giving Inarus was pure wolf. His eyes shimmered metallic silver, a predator locked onto his prey, waiting for it to move before striking.

I made a show of stomping my feet so they'd both know I was there as I walked farther into the room. Neither bothered looking my way. After a second of suspended silence, I marched right over to them and plopped down onto the cool wooden surface of the table between them.

"Hi," I said in a sugary sweet voice.

James raised a brow in my direction. He knew when I got sweet that I was pissed.

"You two done with your pissing contest?" I asked.

Inarus had the decency to look abashed, but James had a wolfish grin on his face that said this was far from over. Yay me.

"No idea what you're talking about, Ari," James said, his grin spreading wide.

I shoved him in the shoulder, disrupting his balancing act and forcing him to rest the chair back on the ground to avoid falling over.

"What was that for?" James asked in mock offense.

I glared at him in response as he chuckled under his breath.

I sighed and shoved off the table, grabbing my belongings as I went. James was watching me, his predatory gaze unwavering. I ignored him and pulled on my boots.

I turned to Inarus. "Thanks for the help. I'll return the clothes later." And then maybe I could just avoid him. Or move. Yeah. I was probably going to have to move.

Dammit.

He nodded.

As I reached for the door, James stood up to follow.

"Aria," Inarus called out.

I turned back to face him.

"We still need to talk."

I nodded. Sure, we'd talk, when hell froze over.

I stalked toward my apartment door with James close on my heels.

"We should talk."

What was up with everyone wanting to talk. I rolled my eyes. If he thought he was going to give me a lecture, he was in for a rude awakening.

"Later." I tried to wave him off as I opened my door.

James frowned but nodded. "I have a few leads to follow on Daniel's case. Nothing concrete and most of it probably a waste of time, but I'm still going to follow through. Get some rest and give me a call when you're feeling better."

I nodded and moved to go inside. Before I could close the door, James moved forward and enveloped me in his arms, nuzzling my hair.

I stiffened for a split second before relaxing into the embrace. "Don't scare me like that again, okay?"

A muffled agreement was all I was able to get out before he released me. His hand rested on my shoulder a moment longer, and he looked me over once more. When he realized I really was fine, he turned to go, leaving me slightly confused yet surprisingly warm inside, in a non-fire-related way.

Chapter Fourteen

I wasn't surprised when Inarus made his way into Sanborn Place. Dressed in low-cut jeans that hugged his hips and a form-fitting black shirt, he looked every bit as attractive as he had the first day we'd met.

Good looks didn't mean I trusted him any farther than I could throw him, though. It's like that saying, "Save my life once, good for you. Save it three times and then maybe I'll trust you." We weren't there yet, and I didn't plan on giving him enough opportunities to get there.

He walked into the office with a casual gait and looked around, taking everything in. I watched him from the corner of my eye as he stopped by Mike's desk and spoke to him for several minutes.

I pretended to be busy, shuffling papers around and typing the same word over and over again on my keyboard when in reality, my attention was solely on him. My skin prickled with awareness, and I wasn't sure if that was a good thing or a bad thing.

My nerves coiled deep in the pit of my stomach and warning

bells blared in my head, telling me that I needed to run. Hide. Get away as fast as possible.

I shook my head. What was wrong with me?

After roughly five minutes, Inarus headed for my desk, done with whatever discussion he'd had with Mike. I kept my gaze locked on the screen of my computer.

"Hey. Can we talk?" He pulled out the chair in front of my desk before taking a seat.

I glanced up and gave him a brief look before focusing my attention back on my work. "Can't. I'm buried in work right now." I shrugged my shoulders while offering a small smile in apology.

"Really? Work, huh?" His tone dripped with skepticism.

"Yup. I'm really behind in paperwork. It'll take me weeks to get caught up."

"You know, I was talking to your boss, Mike …"

I narrowed my eyes at him. Where was he going with this?

"And he said that you'd been complaining all morning about how you didn't have any fresh leads for whatever it is you're working on. How you were bored out of your mind and thinking of taking off early."

I shot an accusing glare in Mike's direction. He had the good sense to turn around and walk to the back of the office, whistling as he went.

Coward.

"Is that so?" I asked in a sugary sweet voice. I was really going to have to remind Mike not to tell complete strangers that I was available. He should know better.

"Mm-hmm," Inarus said. A wide smile spread across his face. The bastard had me, and he knew it.

I heaved a sigh, resigned to my fate, and powered down my computer.

"Let's get this over with." I got up from my seat.

"Don't sound so excited," he chuckled.

I waved a hand over my shoulder and walked outside. The crisp fall air whipped across my cheeks. Looking around, I noted the streets were fairly empty. Few people walked down the sidewalks, and even fewer cars were parked at the surrounding shops. I checked my watch. It was only three in the afternoon. An unusual time for it to be so quiet.

Walking a quick block with Inarus beside me, we made our way to a local coffee shop and bakery.

The door chimed as we walked through it, and the barista quickly greeted us—a young woman in her late teens with bleached-blonde hair and hot pink highlights who stood behind the counter with a wide grin on her face.

She was covered in tattoos, and several facial piercings and dermals adorned her features. Back before the Awakening, things like tattoos and piercings had still been frowned upon. But now, even kids as young as sixteen and as innocent looking as this girl —with her Cupid's bow mouth and baby blue eyes—had them.

God, she looked so young. I wasn't one to judge, though. Even I had a bit of ink.

I'd gotten my first tattoo, the dagger on my right hip, at seventeen. Shortly after the death of my parents. However, the artist that did my tattoo left out the fact that he was a mage with the ability to weave magic into ink and flesh. And he had woven a touch of magic into the blade tattoo, something I'm grateful for to this day, though it hurt like hell. My dagger came to life when I pushed my fingers against the tattoo. In a slow pull of magic, the blade would detach itself from my flesh, becoming solid and unbreakable in my hand. It was a magnificent piece of metal, but its magical qualities made it priceless. I kept it on me at all times, though I chose to use the more traditional daggers I carried sheathed at my hips unless I had no other choice.

When I'd questioned him about it afterward, he'd said he'd known my father. He'd also told me that he knew I was down on my luck.

It was unlike a mage to lend a helping hand. Generosity wasn't something they were known for. They were gamblers and partyers, often found trading magical spells and charms for money or favors on the magical black market.

They often self-medicated with drugs and alcohol as a means of managing the effects of their magic. Mage magic came with a price, and it was usually pain, in spades. But that didn't keep them from pursuing more power and wealth.

Placing my order for a large black coffee, I took my steaming mug to a table in the corner, positioning myself against the wall so I had a good view of the entrance and no one could sneak up behind me.

Inarus followed with his own cup and stood for a moment contemplating where to sit. He frowned when he realized he was going to have to place his back to the entrance, and I filed that tidbit of information away.

Seemed he didn't like leaving himself vulnerable either.

I had just taken a large swallow of my coffee, savoring the flavor, when Inarus dove in to conversation.

"So, what's your story?" He tried to look nonchalant, but the stiff set of his spine and the tight grip on his coffee mug let me know this was far from casual conversation.

I quirked a brow over the edge of my cup and took another drink. Did he really expect me to be so easy? That I would just unfold for him like a book and share my life's story? "Why don't you share yours?" I suggested and turned away to scan the coffeehouse.

The Rocket Bakery was comfortable, cozy even. Filled with mismatched tables and an assortment of upholstered chairs, the strong smell of coffee permeated the air and gave it an inviting atmosphere.

The Rocket Bakery happened to be my favorite coffee shop in town, and they made one heck of a blueberry cream cheese tart. Silently, I debated ordering a slice. Maybe if I were too busy eating, Inarus would take the hint and not ask too many questions.

I eyed him again and sighed. I wouldn't be that lucky, judging by the determined gleam in his eyes.

"Is this going to turn into a 'I'll show you mine if you show me yours first' type of conversation?" he asked me, a sly smile on his face.

I scoffed. "If only you were so lucky."

Letting out a chuckle, Inarus leaned back in his chair and winked at me over the rim of his mug as he took a long pull of his coffee. I watched his throat work, his Adam's apple bobbing as he swallowed before setting the cup aside. "Fine, I'll bite. I'm a psyker like yourself. My abilities manifested when I was eight years old, and I'm what you'd consider a seven on a ten-point scale. Your turn." He said it all very businesslike, as though he were reading stats off the back of a baseball card.

I eyed him skeptically and decided to give him as little information as possible. But a part of me was curious, and I wanted to give him enough that he'd continue with this game and maybe spill something of actual interest. "My abilities manifested when I was thirteen, and I have no idea what level I am. You're the first psyker I've met in person." That I knew of, at least.

"Really?" He was surprised by my answer.

"Yes. Really."

His brows furrowed as he seemed to mull that over for a moment, like psykers were a dime a dozen, and he was astonished that I hadn't run into another before.

I was no expert. But I would hope that if I ran across another psyker, I'd know it. Then again, I'd been avoiding others like me all my life, and I hadn't had any clue that Inarus was telekinetic when I'd first met him in the hallway outside of my apartment.

"Do you know anything about the psyker community?"

I barked out a laugh. Was that supposed to be a trick question? "I do my best to avoid your community."

"Why?" He looked genuinely confused.

I had to fight not to laugh again. He couldn't possibly be that naïve.

If I'd learned anything after the Awakening, it was that everyone looked out for themselves. And those with power stepped on anyone they could to gain more of it. My abilities were different and could be catastrophic in the wrong hands. People lied and manipulated to get what they wanted. Why would I want to mingle with power-hungry paranormals? And there was no doubt in my mind that psykers were just as power hungry as every other faction.

I didn't say any of this out loud, though. Instead I said, "I prefer riding solo."

Inarus pursed his lips together. "You belong with your own people."

"I don't see anything wrong with the people I spend my time with now," I quipped. James, Melody, and Mike were all I needed.

"You have no idea what you're missing. The things you could learn if …"

I held up a hand. "Look, I get it. I'm just not interested."

He frowned. "Aren't you the least bit curious about where you came from? What your full potential is?"

"I know where I came from. I knew both my parents growing up, and no, I don't need to know my full potential. What I'm capable of doing now is enough for me." Well, that wasn't entirely true. Having more control over my pyrokensis would be helpful, but I wasn't going to tell him that.

"Aria, you don't know what you're missing. When psykers get together, amazing things can happen. Just think of all the possibilities. Wouldn't you like to be someplace where you didn't have to hide what you are, what you can do? Where you are respected for your powers? Look, there's this group ..."

As soon as he said group, my attention fixed. I squared my shoulders and gave him my full focus, something prickling, letting me know that this was important.

"It's called PsyShade, and it's a human organization, but psykers are at the heart of it."

Yeah, I'd heard of them before. A few years back when a strange man came knocking on my door. Instantly my hackles rose. This wasn't good.

"You're one of them?" I asked, unable to tone down the accusation in my voice. "You're a part of this group, this PsyShade organization?"

Inarus shook his head. "No, not officially. But," He looked disappointed for a moment before he masked the expression with a smile. "I figured you'd want to know more since people like us run it."

I nodded. It made sense, sure. And yes, I did want to know more. But I didn't want to be a part of anything.

After seeing my initial reaction, Inarus seemed to choose his next words carefully. "I'm going to a gala tonight. Several prominent people in the human and psyker community will be there. Come with me. It'll be good for you to mingle and get to know others like us."

I frowned. "I don't think—"

"You don't have to tell anyone who you are. What you can do. Come in, meet people. See what psykers are really about. Who knows? You might be surprised."

I considered his offer, really considered it. I was interested. I wanted to see this other side that had never been open to me before, but the voice of reason in my head was saying it was a really bad idea. This was the very thing I'd been running from for years. Why wasn't I running now?

Biting my lip, I looked into Inarus's eyes. He offered me a smile, his eyes pleading, and I melted. Dammit.

"Fine," I said under my breath.

"Great," he said, jumping from his seat. "I'll have a dress delivered later this afternoon."

"You don't need to do that."

"Yes, I do. I insist."

I decided not to argue. It's not like gala-ready dresses were something I stockpiled in my closet. The only dress I had was a boring black one meant for funerals, and a leather mini skirt from my younger days, neither of which had been worn in years. Thankfully.

"I have conditions," I told him.

"Name them."

"I'm just an ordinary girl. Not a pyrokinetic."

Inarus smiled mischievously. "Sure. I can go along with that."

I almost reconsidered my decision.

"I'll swing by your apartment at six." He made a hasty retreat before I could change my mind.

❧

AT FIVE THERE WAS A KNOCK AT THE DOOR. A DELIVERY BOY around eighteen or nineteen stood in the doorway when I opened it, his arms full. Two gift bags hung from either arm, with several boxes stacked between them in his outstretched hands.

I lurched forward, reaching for the packages as he wavered in front of me under the weight of his load. "Here, let me take those."

"Thank you," he said, sweat dripping from his brow.

"Did you carry all of this up the stairs?" I asked. "All four flights of them?"

At his nod, I added, "Why didn't you just take the elevator?" Maybe he had a phobia of enclosed spaces like I did.

The boy wiped his sleeve across his forehead as I placed the final bag on the floor just inside my apartment. "There was a woman downstairs. She told me it was out of order."

I attempted a laugh, but my previous injury and my aching ribs would only allow a small giggle to escape.

He gave me a perplexed look, and when I got my painful laughter under control I asked, "Did she happen to have long black hair, green eyes, wings, and was around my height?"

He nodded enthusiastically, a wide grin on his face. "And she was really pretty."

I laughed again. The sound coming out more like a wheeze. Yes, Melody certainly was pretty. "You realize she's a harpy? Right?"

His face grew serious. "My mother taught me that we are all equal—"

I raised a hand, cutting him off. "I wasn't implying that she was unworthy of your attention for being a harpy." I watched as he visibly relaxed his shoulders. What a sweet kid. He was going to defend Mel. Little did he know, she would chew him up and spit him right back out. "What I meant was that she lied. She's a harpy. It's in her nature, and you fell for it. I'm sure she got a kick out of you struggling with all of these packages." I waved a hand to indicate the large pile beside me.

A flush crept up his neck, and for a moment, I felt bad for the guy. It may have been better had I not said anything. "It's okay." I pulled some cash from my pocket and handed it to him. "It happens to the best of us."

His expression wilted.

"Look. Melody only takes the time to screw with guys she thinks are worth her efforts." I leaned in conspiratorially. "You're pretty hot, so I can see why she singled you out."

His eyes brightened, and a flush crept up his cheeks.

"You think I'm—"

"Don't let it go to your head kid." I winked, and with that, I shut the door.

Picking up the packages from the floor, I moved them to my room before delving into their contents. I wasn't really one for dressing up, but as I lifted the lid on one of the gift boxes, exposing a luxurious red dress, I had to appreciate its beauty.

Pulling it out displayed yards of supple fabric. The dress was beautifully draped and sported a high slit and a low-cut back. I set the dress aside and moved to open the rest of the packages.

One of the boxes held a pair of strappy heels in a metallic gold color. They were beautiful and the perfect size.

The shoes were one thing—he likely looked when he helped me remove my boots after the attack. But as I opened the remaining box, I gasped. Lingerie? Oh my god. How the hell had he figured out that sizing?

Inside was a backless red bra with matching underwear and a garter belt, to boot. I shook my head as I pulled each scrap of lace from its package. Lingerie was not something Inarus needed to be purchasing for me.

My cheeks heated as I opened the accompanying card.

> *I figured you'd feel more comfortable with a weapon. This should match better than your daggers and leather sheath.*
> *—Inarus*

I SET THE LINGERIE ASIDE AND PULLED OUT A VELVET POUCH nestled beneath the scraps of lace. Inside was a three-inch silver blade with a finger grip handle. It was shaped like a spearhead but sharper and significantly smoother. Under it was a small black band with a thin slit for the blade to rest in.

I smiled as I held each item in my hands. He'd thought of everything.

Quickly undressing, I opted to wear my own underwear. There had to be boundaries.

I threw on the provided bra and strapped the thin black sheath and blade to the outside of my right thigh.

I slipped into the dress, and sighed at the feel of the lush fabric caressing my skin. Turning, I looked in the mirror above my dresser. The dress hugged my body as if it had been tailored for my shape alone. The halter neckline gave the dress a modest look, but when I turned around, my fully exposed back gave the dress sex appeal that no amount of cleavage could have achieved.

I'd never seen myself look so put together. The blade was hidden perfectly within the dress's floor-length folds, but the high slit provided easy access should I need it.

I chose to put my hair in a high knot on top of my head, exposing the column of my neck in what I hoped to be an attractive fashion. I dabbed a touch of makeup on my face to cover the bruises that still lingered, keeping things light with just a touch of mascara, blush, and lip gloss that I hoped would detract from my split lip.

My bruises were fading at record speed, but my body had prioritized my ribs and internal bruising. Surface wounds would be last to heal. With any luck, they'd be gone within the next few hours.

It wasn't long before I heard a knock at the door and quickly slipped into the provided shoes before answering.

Inarus greeted me in a black suit with a black dress shirt and vest. He was striking, and it took me several moments to gain my composure enough to greet him.

"Hi."

"You look stunning," he told me, and held out his arm.

"You do too," I blurted out. I inwardly cringed.

A wide grin spread across his face.

I couldn't believe I'd said that.

"I meant, thank you." I placed my hand in the crook of his arm. With my free hand, I locked the door behind me and let Inarus escort me out.

He headed towards the elevator, but I shook my head.

He gave me a questioning look but redirected our steps toward the staircase instead.

I eyed the elevator through my peripheral with more disdain than usual. If I face-planted going down these stairs, I was going to put a nice boot-shaped dent in its shiny metal doors.

Chapter Fifteen

On our way to the gala, James called to say that there were no leads regarding our case or my attack. I hadn't expected him to find anything, but the confirmation was still a disappointment.

I assured him I was feeling better and was taking the night off to rest. He didn't need to know I was out with Inarus. Knowing James, he'd show up uninvited, his protective streak taking over.

We drove for an hour before we arrived in Newport and pulled up to a beautiful manor, situated on a hilltop near Diamond Lake with a direct sight line to the water.

The view was breathtaking.

Inarus exited the car and came around to open my door. He held out his arm, and I placed my hand in the crook of his elbow once again, allowing him to lead me inside. Shrubs of varying sizes flanked the walkway leading to wide double doors framed by tall white pillars. The home was wrapped in windows, allowing light from the interior to bleed into the night.

When we walked in, a hostess dressed in a gown I was sure cost more than my yearly salary greeted us just inside the foyer. Inarus handed the woman his invitation. She smiled politely as she matched the name on the invitation with her list, then ushered us in.

The venue was beautiful on the outside, but inside, it was magnificent. Marble floors went on endlessly throughout. The walls were painted a soft grey, and chandeliers dotted the ceiling, illuminating the entire space in a warm, ethereal glow.

Inarus led me farther inside as though he were familiar with the place. Past the entry and through a wide hall, we made our way into what appeared to be a banquet room. The lights were dimmed, casting faint shadows along the walls. Tables were spread throughout, with eight chairs situated around each one. The room was bustling with activity. Finely dressed men and women with glasses of champagne in their hands greeted one another and made quiet conversation.

On the far side of the room was a small stage and podium, currently unoccupied. Hmm. I wondered what was discussed at an event like this. Inarus didn't mention if it were just a dinner or a ceremony of some sort. But it was clear that someone would be giving a speech.

Inarus guided me to a table on our left with his palm resting on the small of my back. He pulled out my chair, and I took a seat, grateful for the opportunity to rest my feet. The shoes he'd given me were beautiful but a killer to walk in.

His hand brushed my hip as he helped to scoot my chair in closer, and small tingles ran up my spine. Gah, what was wrong with me?

I muttered curses under my breath as he excused himself to grab a few drinks, giving me the chance to take in my surroundings and catch my breath. His proximity was getting to me, and the casual touches were heightening my nerves. Every time he placed his hand on the small of my back or reached for my hand to guide me, goose bumps broke out across my skin.

I wondered if he noticed my reaction to him. God, I hoped

not. How humiliating would that be? I'd never felt so on edge before just by the presence of a man.

I rubbed my arms and casually glanced around the room.

Voices to my right caught my attention, and I found myself staring at a couple in a heated conversation. The man's face was red in anger, and the woman was frantically wiping moisture from her eyes as he spoke to her in an abrupt tone. I strained to hear what they were saying but only caught bits and pieces.

"Don't you dare—"

"Do you have any idea the things—"

"Know your place." The man stood to leave the table.

As soon as he rose from his seat, I got a better view of the woman, and was shocked to see someone I recognized. Jessica Blackmore sat two tables away, dabbing at her eyes with a napkin as her husband stalked off toward the French doors that led outside. She waved over a waiter and took a glass of champagne from his serving tray. In a matter of seconds, Jessica downed the champagne, then took another from the same server's tray. She downed the second just like the first.

I stared in surprise, unsure what I was witnessing. Jessica was visibly upset, and I wondered what the cause was. What had she and Patrick Blackmore been arguing about? Did it have to do with Daniel?

Curiosity got the better of me, and when Jessica rose from her seat, I moved to follow.

She headed to the ladies' room, and I hurried to keep up with her in my ridiculously high heels. Tonight may have started off as a social event, but it might turn into a lead. Jessica grabbed more champagne on her way, retrieving two glasses this time from a server that crossed her path. Downing the first in her hand she placed the empty glass on a side table as she entered the bathroom.

I glanced around to make sure no one was watching, then slipped through the door behind her. I flicked the lock to make sure we weren't interrupted—and to slow her down if she refused to speak to me.

Three stalls greeted me. The first two were wide open, displaying their vacancy. The third was closed, and I could just make out Jessica's plum-colored heels beneath the door. I went to the sink and busied myself washing my hands in an attempt to appear casual when she came out.

When the toilet flushed and the door opened, I looked up in the mirror and watched Jessica stumble forward, glass of champagne still in hand. She hadn't noticed yet that she wasn't alone, and when she looked up, her glazed expression locked on mine.

She dropped her glass, and the sound of it shattering echoed in the room.

"What are you doing here?" she slurred. She stepped over the shattered remains of glass, her heels crunching in the debris as she came closer.

I turned on the faucet, washing my hands again while she glared at me in the mirror. I ignored her. Reaching to the right, I retrieved a paper towel and dried my hands.

Her foot tapped expectantly as I finished.

"I'm on a date," I told her. I wasn't sure how to play this, but I had an inkling that she had a secret that was eating at her and she needed to tell someone. I tossed the paper towel in the nearby waste bin and turned to face her, my expression nonchalant.

Jessica's eyes narrowed, her gaze accusing. I kept my expression casual and waited for her to crack. Women like Jessica wanted people to feel sorry for them, and right now, she was a mess. Mascara ran down her cheeks, the black streaks marring her near-perfect skin. If I gave her enough time, she'd tell me what I wanted to know all on her own.

"You … you just think you're so much better than me, don't you? Like you're blessed or something because you can"—she waved her hands in the air—"do things. Well, you're not."

Do things? She couldn't know I was a pyrokinetic, but maybe she assumed I had some other magical ability. It wasn't uncommon for me to be mistaken for a witch or a mage. Most people in my line of work had some type of magical ability. You needed one to survive as a mercenary.

Like I expected, Jessica cracked. I almost smiled.

"What are you talking about? I don't think I'm any better than you are." I didn't want to appear combative. She needed a friend. Someone to confide in. Not an enemy.

The alcohol was clearly having an effect on her coherency. "Oh, don't play dumb. You're better than that, Ms. Naveed. I can tell you're one of them. That glow you have to your eyes. I'm not stupid. I've been around enough of your kind to know."

"I have no idea what you're talking about."

Jessica laughed. "God, how dumb do you think I am? You're at their damn event. You're a psyker, but you know what? I'm on to your guys' little game. You may have my husband fooled, but not me. You all say you're human, like the rest of us. That you're here to help us make things the way they were before, but you're no better. No better than every other non-human abomination that has plagued our world since the Awakening."

Ice filled my veins at the realization that she knew what I was, but I brushed it off. She was drunk. With any luck, she wouldn't remember our conversation come morning. Her prejudice had me taken aback though. Her son was one of these non-human abominations she was referring to.

"Jessica," I said in a calming tone. "I think maybe you've had a little too much to drink."

"Don't judge me," she slurred. "You even look like her, you know that? That stupid bitch, Viola. She took everything from me."

Before I could stop her, Jessica slammed her fist into the mirror. The glass splintered in a web-like pattern. She slammed her fist into it again, small pieces breaking away and clattering to the countertop and floor.

"Shit." I hadn't taken her for the violent type. I grabbed her hand before she was able to hit the mirror again, rivulets of blood dripping down her forearm from her injured hand. "Jessica, stop!"

"She took everything. Everything." She was sobbing now, clutching her bloodied hand to her chest, the crimson liquid staining her dress.

I hastily grabbed paper towels, shoving a wad in her hand to staunch the flow of blood.

Jessica jerked away from me. Her tears gone in a flash, and only anger left behind. "Don't touch me," she all but snarled. "I don't need help from the likes of you. Tell Viola she can rot. I won't allow her to ruin my life any longer."

She tried to storm out of the restroom, but the lock held her up.

"Ahhh!" She kicked the door and cursed.

"Let me help." I moved to flick the lock.

Jessica glowered at me before she jerked it open and stormed out.

I stood there, stunned, and tried to wrap my head around what she'd said. None of it made any sense. I didn't know where to even begin deciphering what had just happened.

I took a deep breath, pulled out my phone from my small clutch, and sent Mike a quick message asking that he look into an organization called PsyShade and a woman connected to it by the name of Viola. He didn't immediately respond, but I knew he'd get the message. I sent James a similar message. Two heads on this were better than one.

Seconds later, James responded, and I knew I was in trouble. I'd forgotten that I'd told him I was taking the night off.

Where are you?

I sent a non-committal message letting him know that I'd

stumbled on a lead but was still taking things easy, and not to worry. Hopefully that would mollify him for the night.

Tucking my phone away, I exited the ladies' room and ran smack into a wall of solid flesh. Inarus steadied me with a hand on my elbow and a smile in his eyes. "We have to stop meeting this way."

A flush of heat crept up my cheeks, and I turned away to hide the blush.

"I was wondering where you'd gone off to."

"Sorry. Just made a quick trip to the ladies' room."

He handed me a glass of champagne, and I took a cautious sip. Having seen its effects on Jessica, I decided to take it easy on the alcohol tonight.

I scanned the room, looking to see if she was still around, but she was nowhere to be seen. Inarus led me back to our table, and we took our seats. I fidgeted beside him.

He leaned in close. "I'm glad you came with me this evening."

I tried to smile. "Me, too." Hopefully he wouldn't realize my unease. What had Jessica meant when she'd said I'd looked just like Viola?

Before either of us could say another word, the lights in the room dimmed further, grabbing everyone's attention.

"Ladies and gentlemen," a voice called. I searched the podium and saw a woman, brightly lit, on the stage. The spotlight was so bright that it was difficult to see what she looked like aside from the floor-length emerald dress she wore and the fall of rich brown hair cascading around her shoulders in loose curls.

"Thank you all for joining us this evening. I wanted to take a moment to welcome you. We will have dinner served shortly, but until then, please mingle."

She exited to the right of the stage, her back now to me.

Something about her was oddly familiar. I craned my neck

over the sea of guests in an effort to get a better look, but each time I got a clear line she was faced away.

Something tugged at me. I needed to see what she looked like. Was this the woman Jessica had mentioned? Jessica seemed to think she was responsible for ruining her life. Could she have been involved in Daniel's murder?

"What are you looking at?" Inarus asked.

"Oh. Sorry. That woman over there." I waved in her direction. "She looked familiar, but I can't get a good look at her. Do you know her?"

He nodded. "Her name is Viola Reynolds. She's on the council for the Human Alliance Corporation."

"The what?" I asked. Since when was there a Human Alliance Corporation? Just the thought of it made me shiver with past thoughts of the KKK and other prejudicial groups.

Inarus let out a laugh. "If you could see the look on your face. It isn't some anti-paranormal group, if that is what you're thinking. The HAC is just an organization that looks out for the rights and safety of all humans. The human population is at a bit of a disadvantage, don't you think?"

I mulled that over for a moment. "I suppose," I said, reluctantly. There was something about it that just didn't sit well. My skin itched with the feeling that there was more to it. Call me paranoid, but historically, when a large group of united individuals assembled, shit hit the fan.

But I decided not to prod. If I attacked him with questions now, he'd clam up. Better to let him believe it wasn't a big concern of mine. If he got comfortable with me and was convinced I thought they were a benefit to the community, perhaps he'd share more information. Information freely given was always more truthful than when pried out of someone.

Inarus and I ate dinner. We laughed and joked about inconsequential topics. He introduced me to a few guests, and I smiled politely and shook their hands. For the most part, I enjoyed myself. A few suspicious glances made my hackles rise but in general, things remained light and casual.

I knew the event had a fair amount of psykers in attendance, but I couldn't pick anyone out from the sea of humans. My experiences with psykers, aside from Inarus, were nil.

Even though I had a decent handle on my abilities, having the opportunity to speak with someone who shared my pyrokinesis and had mastered it, or at the very least maintained control over it, would be useful.

Maybe I'd ask Inarus if he could point out others like me.

"Follow me." Inarus led me away from the couple we'd been speaking with. "I want to introduce you to someone."

I nodded and followed along like a good date. My feet were aching, and I was ready for the night to end. Fancy dinners were not really my thing, but I could meet one more person before we called it a night. Maybe he'd planned to introduce me to another pyrokinetic after all, and I wouldn't have to ask.

We waded through the crowd and offered a smile and casual hello to passersby along our way. We approached a couple deep in conversation. The woman's back was to us, but I recognized her dress and the fall of brown hair as the woman who had spoken at the podium. The woman who Inarus had said was Viola Reynolds.

She was laughing at something the man had just said, and the sound inspired a smile on my face. We were about ten yards away when she turned to speak to an approaching woman, and I froze.

Inarus kept walking, but my feet refused to move. My chest grew tight, and my breathing became labored and choppy as though I'd just run a marathon.

Time stood still as I watched the woman before me. Small wrinkles formed at the corners of her eyes as she smiled. She looked happy. Ecstatic even.

I wanted to run to her. To throw my arms around her and cry in her embrace. She was here. She was alive. I couldn't believe it.

Inarus called my name, but I ignored him. My gaze focused solely on my mother, the woman I'd believed dead for the past six years. I knew she was my mother. It didn't matter that she used a different name. Deep down, I knew exactly who she was.

Her laugh was the same, and it took me back to my childhood.

A million questions ran through my mind. What was she doing here? Why was she going by Viola Reynolds when her real name was Victoria Naveed? Why had she left me?

The last question made me pause. I knew my mother. She had raised me, loved me, and she'd loved my father. She would never have left willingly.

I wanted to steal her away. Rescue her. Because why else would she be here, away from me, if she didn't need to be rescued? But reality set in. Something wasn't right.

Inarus had said she was on the council for the Human Alliance Corporation. She wasn't just my mother. She was important to these people, to their cause.

When Inarus reached her, he placed a hand on her elbow and gestured in my direction. She offered him a small smile, then turned her head towards me. Time moved at a snail's pace as she turned, her hair brushing over her shoulder, and her eyes slowly roved over the crowd, searching for the person Inarus was pointing at. Me.

I panicked and turned away. I couldn't let her see me, not until I had this figured out. Not until I knew why she had left. How she was still alive.

I forced my feet to move and walked away from her and Inarus.

Inarus called my name again, but I ignored him and ran as fast as my heels would take me. I refused to chance a look over my shoulder.

The cool breeze hit me as I exited the building. I ran down

the front steps and rushed to a nearby yellow cab. I jerked the door open and slid into the back seat.

"Cab's reserved, lady. You'll have to call another one," the driver said.

"I'll double your rate if you get me out of here." I sucked in breath after breath. I needed to calm down before I started to hyperventilate.

The cabbie eyed me through the rearview mirror before giving a tight nod. He pulled out of the circular driveway, and all of the tension trickled out of me. I looked back through the rear window as we made our escape and saw Inarus on the porch steps, a concerned expression on his face.

I couldn't worry about him right now. I just ... I needed to get the hell out of there.

I didn't know where to go. I couldn't go home right now. It was the first place Inarus would look for me, assuming he chose to follow. Dressed as I was, I couldn't go hangout at the coffee shop either. I checked my phone and saw I had a message from Mike telling me he'd dug up some information and that he'd be at the office late.

Perfect.

I gave the cabbie the address to my office, and an hour later he dropped me off. Sanborn Place was a stout brick building in the heart of downtown Spokane. It was on the rougher side of town, nestled between a bakery and a dry cleaner. We had a private parking lot, though, so the building was perfect in my book.

I handed the cabbie a wad of bills I'd tucked into my thigh holster behind my blade and stepped out of the car. I hoped Mike had answers for me, because this was getting more and more twisted as time passed.

Chapter Sixteen

Mike met me at the door with a steaming mug of coffee and a surprised look on his face.

It was the fancy dress.

"I had a thing. It wasn't a big deal." I reached for the mug and ignored his questioning glance. I practically inhaled the coffee as I followed him over to his desk, kicking off my heels along the way. "So, what did you find?"

Mike's expression turned grim as he sat back in his chair. "Ari, I'm not sure how to tell you this but …"

"She's my mother," I blurted out.

His eyes met mine and shock colored his expression. "How did you know?"

"I saw her in person. She was at the gala, and I was maybe ten yards away from her." I waved my hands in the air as I spoke. God, I'd been so close to her.

Mike shook his head and furrowed his brows. "Did you talk to her?"

"Of course not. I panicked. I froze when I realized it was really her, and then before she saw me, I ran away and took a cab straight here."

I saw pity in Mike's eyes, and it made my chest ache that much more. I didn't want his pity.

"Why didn't you talk to her? Ari, maybe she could have answered some questions. Maybe she had a reason?" As he said it, I could tell he didn't believe his own words.

"Mike, what was I supposed to say? 'Hey Mom, it's me. You know, your daughter that you abandoned. What's up?'"

I plopped down in one of Mike's reception chairs and held the cup of coffee to my chest, letting the warmth seep into me. My hands were shaking.

"Ari, I'm so sorry."

"It's okay. It isn't your fault she left me." I felt like an idiot missing her all these years. I was shaking my head, my mind filled with disbelief. How could she be alive? Did that mean my papa—?

No. I'd seen him die. I'd seen the light leave his eyes. There wasn't any coming back from that.

"What if she had reasons for—?" Mike said.

"There isn't a single reason good enough for abandoning your only child. My father was murdered right in front of me, my mother dragged away screaming. I held my father, helpless to do anything but watch him die. And then I was alone. Terrified and alone. And where was my mother? All these years I believed she was dead, too. They took her to another room. I heard her screams. I heard the gunshot before everything went quiet. If she was alive, why didn't she ever come back for me?"

Mike stared at me for several moments. I knew he was at a loss for words, and that was okay. There wasn't anything he could say to make any of this better. Right now, I just wanted whatever information he'd been able to dig up.

"What else were you able to find?"

He sighed and pulled out a small stack of papers from his top desk drawer. "I spoke with a few of our guys on the streets."

I waited for him to continue and took another sip of coffee. "Twitch?"

He nodded. Twitch was a source we frequently used. He was a bit eccentric and leaned towards nervous and paranoid. But he had connections that covered all of Washington and most of Idaho. He was good. Better than good. I wasn't surprised that he was the one Mike had gone to for information.

"Viola Reynolds popped up on the grid five years ago with the founding of the Human Alliance Corporation. She's a council member but carries the deciding vote in all arguments. Think of her as the head of the snake, because that's what the HAC is. The Human Alliance is a front for a new government. Twitch says that their driving goal is to eliminate what they consider to be a threat to humanity and to reinstate a national government."

"They want to destroy the paranormal community?"

He nodded.

"And how does PsyShade factor into all of this?"

"I'm getting to that part."

I smiled. Mike was always one for dramatics. Currently, humans outnumbered paranormals nearly three hundred to one. That didn't mean much, though, when a single rogue vampire could level a city block in a matter of minutes.

"Do we know why they want to eliminate the paranormal community?"

Mike shook his head. "Nothing concrete. Twitch claims that the HAC believes paranormals are an abomination. That their souls are damned, and it's their job to eliminate them."

"Great. They're a bunch of fanatics."

"Pretty much."

This certainly wasn't looking good. "Do you know anything else?"

Mike slid a photo to me. The image was of a man in a long trench coat. He was standing in the middle of a road, arms lifted up with an expression of concentration on his face. Behind him, several cars were floating in the air.

"Are we sure this is real?" I asked.

Mike nodded. "Yeah, here's another one." The second photograph he slid over was of the same man, wearing the same coat. This time he was standing in front of a shop window, unaware of the photographer. Three metal spheres hovered above his palm.

Inarus?

"From what I've gathered, PsyShade and the HAC work hand-in-hand. HAC is the political face, clean and shiny for the public. PsyShade is more covert and does the dirty work at the direction of the HAC."

I stared at each image side by side. The man's face was unrecognizable, hidden in shadow in both pictures. For all I knew, the spheres could be a habit for people with telekinetic abilities, but my neck was prickling. Coincidences were rare.

"Is he linked to the organization?" I asked.

Mike's eyebrows furrowed. "I'm not entirely sure, but I think so."

I sank further into my chair. Of course, Inarus couldn't be some do-gooder in the psyker community. He had to be a radical nutcase who wanted to eradicate the paranormal population. Just my luck.

"Why isn't the HAC interested in also eliminating psykers?" I indicated the photographs.

"Psykers consider themselves to be an advanced version of a human. I spoke with Twitch, and he found this report for me."

"You mean he stole this report for you," I corrected.

Mike had the decency to look chastened as he handed over the supposed report. I skimmed the paper quickly. It listed similarities between two strands of DNA.

"Where is this from?"

"A research lab in Seattle compared the DNA of a normal

human to that of a psyker. They're a match. With vampires, you find a third DNA strand. No one knows why it's there or what it means, but every vampire has one. In shifters, we see an increase in chromosomes due to the Lyc-V virus. It alters their DNA structure after infection and alters their very chemical makeup. Harpies lack three chromosomes and the Fae—well, who knows? I doubt anyone has ever been close enough to study one, but it's safe to say that they're different from humans in DNA structure and makeup. Psykers though, according to this report, are the same. Identical genetic makeup as a regular human being, though this report also lists an increase in healing capabilities. I'm sure there are other differences, but their DNA makeup is, in fact, the same."

It was comforting in a strange way. I'd always considered myself human, but at the same time, I was afraid of what might happen if someone got a sample of my blood. What would they find? What would they suspect? These questions constantly plagued me, but now I could at least set them aside and be thankful for the rapid healing abilities. I had a feeling they'd continue to come in handy.

Endless questions began streaming through me. Was the HAC a threat? Obviously, they were if they wanted to eliminate the paranormal community. But how big of a role did psykers play in this? Was I the lone psyker outside of PsyShade? Maybe that was why I'd never run into another before.

My thoughts turned to Inarus. He'd been growing on me, but after this, I wasn't so sure. What if he was the man in the photos? Did it matter? They didn't incriminate him of anything, they were just recordings of his abilities. Right?

That prickle on the back of my neck was warning me, and I could see red flags popping up all over the place. He had taken me to the gala to introduce me to the psyker community. Viola —I couldn't even think of her as my mother—was on the council for the Human Alliance Corporation. Inarus had said he wanted to teach me more about psykers. If psykers had no connection to the HAC, then why was he so insistent I go to that event?

"I ran into Jessica Blackmore," I blurted out. I wasn't sure why, but what she'd said suddenly seemed important. "She was drunk."

"Did you talk to her? What did she say?"

"She was angry. She ranted on about how Viola had taken everything from her. She called paranormals an abomination. It struck me as odd since Daniel was a shifter, but I'm wondering if Jessica was involved. If she'd somehow played a role in Daniel's death without realizing it, or if when she did, it was already too late."

"What is your gut telling you?" he asked.

"That my mother isn't the woman I remember."

Mike's expression was solemn. "Ari, have you ever wanted to, you know, find out more about people like yourself?"

I started to shake my head but caught myself. Of course, I wanted to know more about psykers. I wanted to know everything, but it wasn't worth the risk. When I'd been approached before, I'd known it was a set-up, and I'd run. This time, it felt just as tainted.

Nothing was making sense, and my mother coming into the picture was just another monkey wrench in my already existing train wreck of an investigation. I didn't believe in coincidences, and I knew Mike didn't either.

"Not like this. This isn't right, and you know it."

"But what if it is? What if this is your chance?"

"No. I don't believe that, and you don't either, not really."

He nodded.

"Mike, there's something else I should tell you." I stood up and paced. Pulling the silver dagger from my thigh sheath, I thoughtlessly flipped it through my fingers. I fumbled for the right words to say. I didn't know if he was my enemy. I really didn't want him to be, but I couldn't ignore what was in front of me, either. Not if it put Mike at risk.

"Ari, just come out with it. You're making me nervous, and stop flinging that thing around. You're going to hurt yourself."

I sheathed my blade and stopped pacing. Placing both hands down on the front of Mike's desk, I leaned forward and stared him straight in the eyes. "That guy in the picture."

"Yeah, what about him?"

"I'm pretty sure he's the same guy I just went on a date with. The one you met the other day when you sent him over to my desk."

Mike swore. I pushed off the desk and sat back down.

"He's a psyker too?"

I nodded. "He's a telekinetic." I indicated the pictures between us. "I've seen him with spheres just like these."

Mike nodded. "And your mother."

I cringed. I didn't know who she was anymore, but I was pretty sure mother was a title she no longer carried. Shaking my head, I answered, "Not that I know of. I never saw her display any psyker abilities growing up, and she was well aware of mine. If she was a psyker, I don't think she would have kept it from me."

"We need to figure out how all of this plays into Daniel's death. If their goal is to eliminate the paranormal community, the easiest way to accomplish that is to have paranormals destroy themselves."

"Did you just say 'we' need to figure it out?"

"Of course I did. I'm not leaving you to handle this all on your own. You're in way over your head," he chided me.

"I've got James. The entire Pack as well if I need them."

He scoffed. "Not good enough."

I let it go, knowing this was just Mike having my back. I told him about Emma and the dead vampire James and I had been called to investigate, leaving out my close call. There wasn't any reason to worry him further. I'd concealed my injuries well enough that he wouldn't notice on his own.

Mike agreed that something fishy was going on. The knowledge that psykers and the HAC were around gave us both a feeling they'd had a hand in the deaths. We just needed to follow the breadcrumbs.

A part of me was frustrated with myself for not having heard of the HAC before. I prided myself on knowing secrets, and this was information I should have been aware of. Despite our vast resources, and even with Mike and James's help, I was going to need more if we were going to get to the bottom of this.

We had no proof that psykers or the HAC were involved with either crime. Only an inkling of suspicion, and that wasn't enough. On top of that, even if they were responsible, the HEPD would do nothing about it. Paranormals policed their own, and I didn't remember my mother ever being reckless. She wasn't stupid. If she played any part in this, her hands would be clean. No, someone else did the dirty work.

I needed to call James.

Chapter Seventeen

The following morning, I pulled up to the Pack Compound. It was thirty minutes by car out of Spokane and nestled on one hundred and seven acres of forested property. I drove my little Civic up to the looming wooden gates.

The Compound building was surrounded by a fifteen-foot fence constructed out of large grey bricks and mortar. The thing was solid and imposing, and I had a feeling that even though the fence was there to keep outsiders from getting in, I'd have one hell of a time getting out if something went wrong.

My hands gripped the steering wheel more firmly as the double doors groaned, slowly opening. I crept my car forward and took in my surroundings.

The structure that looked impressive from the outside was downright daunting as I drove through its gates. Its height was nothing in comparison to its girth. The wall stood at least a foot deep. There was no way I'd be able to go over it, certainly not through it, and if I had to guess, the shifters had ensured that no one could pass under it either. They had built themselves a pretty little fortress.

Driving farther, I found myself following a winding path

surrounded by enormous evergreens. After five minutes, the Compound itself finally came into view. It was a fortress constructed from large stone blocks, heavily protected and fortified. The perimeter was teeming with activity. I counted over a dozen shifters on patrol, and those were only the ones I could see from my current position.

The shifters had successfully created what appeared to be an impenetrable building, and I was positive that whatever weakness the Compound held, it was diligently monitored and patrolled at all times.

I parked my car and sat for several moments, trying to rein in my emotions and remember every detail I knew about the Pack and its Alpha.

The Alpha of the Pacific Northwest shifters was none other than Declan Valkenaar. He was a white Bengal tiger, and in human form he had nearly white hair and startling emerald eyes. In tiger form, his coat was snow white with stripes the deepest shade of black.

How did I know this? I found him on Wikipedia. Not all information is found by sleuthing through darkened streets.

I also knew that he led the Pacific Northwest Pack, which encompassed all of Washington, Oregon, Idaho, and parts of Montana. He's yet to be challenged, and that fact alone scared the hell out of me.

Alphas were typically challenged almost every year. To be unopposed for nine consecutive years meant one of two things, either he was one scary sonovabitch and no one thought they could take him, or he was the perfect leader and everyone was happy with his rule. I'd lay odds that of the two, the former was true. About the latter, I had no idea. Yet.

Finally mustering the courage to leave my vehicle, I opened the door and made sure to keep my face devoid of any expression. "Cool as a cucumber", that was my motto today. As I walked toward the main doors, two shifters, a man and a woman, approached.

Babysitters. Yay me.

The man was a tank—short and stocky and wrapped in cords of muscle. His black fatigues and buzz cut screamed former military. The woman, on the other hand, was petite and delicate in her pale blue sundress and strappy gold sandals. Her straight blonde hair blew in the breeze, and I had to bite my cheek to keep from grinning.

She had honest-to-god freckles and looked like she should be on a cheerleading squad, not out here greeting me on the pack grounds. She was so damn tiny I couldn't imagine what she shifted into.

The man was a bear without a doubt. He may not have been tall, but he was thick and walked like a rhinoceros stomping through the mud.

"Welcome to the Compound. I'm Jennifer, and this is Mauro. We will be your guides," the woman said in a singsong voice.

I inclined my head in thanks and followed them into the Compound.

The hallways were wide. Several shifters walked past me, ignoring my presence as if I didn't exist. Not that I wanted them to notice me, but still, a simple "hello" or "excuse me" would have been nice.

I continued to follow my appointed guides down the labyrinth of hallways, my boots making soft thumping noises with each step. Despite Mauro's size, his footsteps were silent, as were Jennifer's. I cringed over the ruckus I was making. How the hell were they able to remain silent when I sounded like I was stomping on bricks? Maybe it was the shoes? More likely, though, was that the flooring had been engineered to make noise.

Shifters moved silently with little to no effort. They were predators, and stealth was in their very nature. I, on the other hand, had not been given that gift. Obviously.

Turning a sharp corner, Jennifer opened a set of double doors that led to a staircase. I looked up. They were practically never ending. Just what I needed. More damn stairs. It wasn't like I could ever have enough of those.

Seven steps up, Jennifer paused and looked down at me. "Do you need an elevator?"

I shook my head. I would have loved to take an elevator, really I would. Only I'd turn into a five-year-old having a meltdown. So, unfortunately, the never-ending stairs it would be.

She nodded and continued making her way up as I followed, Mauro already a full flight above us.

On the fifth flight, my lungs began to burn. By the sixth, sweat was dripping from my brow and between my breasts. Wonderful. These shifters would be able to smell me a mile away. Gross.

By the seventh floor, I had to grit my teeth and push my legs forward by sheer force of will. I would not be seen as weak. I would climb these damn stairs, and I would not take a break.

When we reached the eighth floor, we finally stopped. Mauro reached forward and gripped the door handle leading out of the stairwell.

An audible sigh of relief exited my mouth. I turned my head from left to right to loosen the tension in my shoulders, the pop of my neck audible in the silence. There was nothing I could do for the stiffness in my legs, though. Not here, anyway.

I was led down yet another hallway, this one bathed in amber lighting. The bare walls were made of simple stone, and doorways lined either side. At the end, it branched off in two directions. We turned to our right and followed it down to a lone doorway. Two shifters were posted outside the door, standing guard. Each wore jeans and a black shirt. Nothing as dramatic as the black fatigues Mauro wore, but they still held a military presence.

I was beginning to get the idea that none of them had

actually served, rather they were just combat-trained and always at the ready. A personal army for the Pack.

Jennifer nodded towards both men, and they nodded to her in kind. She opened the door and ushered me through. I took a deep breath and steeled myself before I walked in.

Here goes nothing.

The room was large and structured like a small auditorium. The outer edges were raised with four rows of elevated benches. Seating for an audience. In the center of the room was a large rectangular wooden table surrounded by seventeen chairs. Eight on either side and one chair at the end.

Standing next to that chair, at the head of the table, was Declan. I could tell by his platinum white hair and emerald green eyes that he was the Pack's Alpha, but what I hadn't gathered from the pictures online was just how imposing he was in person.

The room was large, but he loomed larger. Over six feet tall with muscles that looked carved from stone. He had an angular jaw and a sharp slash of lips. Thick brows gave him a hooded expression, but his eyes were what truly captivated my attention. They were twin jewels that glittered in the light, and they were currently narrowed in my direction.

"Lucky me." Shit, I'd said that aloud. So much for first impressions.

I made my way farther into the room and quickly assessed the other individuals. Aside from Mauro and Jessica, who were currently behind me, and Declan, who stood ahead, there were five others. Two women and three men.

As I approached, each eyed me with varying levels of hostility as they stood next to their chair. I took it to mean they didn't appreciate a human meddling in their business but didn't really care what their thoughts on the matter were.

Both women were on Declan's right. The first had an exotic appearance—bronzed skin, brown eyes, and an ebony mane that fell in waves to her waist. She was dressed in casual denim jeans and a solid red T-shirt.

The woman beside her was almost her complete opposite—creamy skin, cold, calculating eyes, and copper-colored hair pulled into a tight bun on top of her head. She wore jeans as well, along with a white T-shirt that dipped low, displaying her ample cleavage.

I could tell right away that she'd already added me to her shit list, and I hadn't even introduced myself.

Across the table, the men stood behind their respective chairs. They each looked like they could easily bench press a thousand pounds. These guys were stacked, and I do mean stacked. Two of them were surely brothers, if not twins. Their features were almost identical. Both had bronze skin, dark brown eyes, military-short hair, and tribal tattoos adorning their bare arms.

Interesting. Maybe when the case was closed, I'd do a little digging and see if there was a meaning behind the tats.

The third man at the table had blond hair and blue eyes. His olive skin and sprinkling of facial hair gave him a roguish look, but without the facial hair he'd be boy-band pretty. His features were clearly defined. High cheekbones and a small, but sharp nose. If he wanted to, even in our current society, he could have easily been a model. He was that good looking.

When I reached the edge of the table I stopped, waiting to see what would happen next. I knew more about how the Pack operated than I should, and that knowledge made me aware of the fact that there was a very strict sense of order. Their position in relation to Declan meant something, and I didn't want to fumble this and take the wrong seat.

So I waited. Patiently. Or at least as patiently as I was capable of, which really wasn't saying much.

Jennifer and Mauro walked past me, then each stood behind a seat. Jennifer to the right of the copper-haired woman, and

Mauro to the right of Jennifer. With everyone in place aside from me, Declan finally spoke.

"Welcome to the Compound." His voice boomed in the enclosed space.

I attempted a smile. "Thanks for having me."

He nodded and continued. Pointing to his left, he began making introductions. Indicating the exotic-looking woman he began, "Not all of the Pack's Alphas were able to make our meeting. however, a representative from each pack is here. This is Eva Padilla, female Alpha of the Feloidea." He didn't bother explaining what that meant, but I knew Clan Feloidea encompassed hyenas, mongooses, and civets.

"Beside her is Yvonne Mendez, Alpha of Clan Muridea." The rodent Clan. "Jennifer, whom you've already met, along with her mate Mauro, are the Betas of Clan Bear."

Whoa, didn't see that one coming. I mean sure, Mauro I figured for a bear, but Jennifer, she was less than a third of his size. I just couldn't picture it.

"To my left," Declan continued, "are Tegan and Derek Keen, joint Alphas of Clan Wolf, and last is Robert Yazzie, Alpha of Clan Canidae."

Canidae were foxes, jackals, and coyotes. Robert flashed me a feral grin. I was pretty sure he was a coyote. When he smiled, he took on a manic look, giving me goosebumps all along my arms. I did not want to find myself in an empty stairwell with him. Good looking or not.

"I am the Pack's Alpha, and leader of Clan Cat," Declan continued. "Please, take a seat." He indicated the seat beside Robert, and inwardly I cringed. If he bit me, I was going to bite back, and then light his ass on fire for good measure.

Declan took his seat, and the rest of us followed.

Just as I sat, the door I'd previously entered through opened, and in walked James. I exhaled a sigh of relief. I was wondering if he would show up, and having him here helped set my nerves at ease.

James inclined his head in greeting toward Declan before taking a seat beside me. I resisted the urge to move my seat closer to his and farther from Robert. Instead I folded my hands on the table's wooden surface and waited for Declan to continue.

"As many of you know, James has brought to our attention, through his work with Ms. Naveed, that we have a third party in our midst that is trying to cause a war between the Pack and the Coven. Our relationship with the Coven is subtly hostile at best, but it will not benefit either side if we go to war."

Several heads were nodding in agreement, but one, in particular, seemed to disagree.

"The vampires are not our friends. They're our enemy, and war is imminent. That has never been a secret. Why bother preventing the inevitable? Our numbers have grown over the years. In the end, we would prevail." Eva was smiling as several grunts of agreement sounded.

I stared at the beautiful brunette, wondering if she were dense.

"That may be true," Declan said. "We would likely be the victors. However," He paused, making eye contact with each individual at the table. "Our casualties would be in the hundreds, and when the dust settled, we would be vulnerable to further attacks. There is a third player on the board. We know little about them or what they are. What we do know is that they want our city. If the Pack and the Coven go to war, we open the streets for whoever they are to waltz right through town and take what we fought for. We would lose."

Declan's announcement brought on a stir of murmuring and a variety of facial expressions—ranging from deeply worried to outright disbelief—from the normally stoic shifters.

I understood their skepticism. They'd just been told, with no proof mind you, that a mysterious group was gunning for them.

They had no reason to believe that there was anyone else out there, aside from the vampires, that posed a threat to them. In their minds, no one else had the numbers and strength to take them on.

"Ms. Naveed, would you care to explain our situation?" he asked, and then went on to offer a quick introduction. "Ms. Naveed has been working with James to bring down the individual responsible for murdering Daniel Blackmore. While following leads, she uncovered some disturbing revelations."

I looked to James, and he smiled in encouragement. We had already discussed our plan of action last night after I had left Sanborn Place. James had immediately decided a meeting with Declan and the Pack Alphas was our best course of action, and I had no reason to disagree. Taking a deep breath, I faced the Pack leaders and laid everything out.

"We originally thought a vampire was responsible for Daniel's death."

"And now?" Declan asked.

I shook my head. "I spoke with Rebecka. She's arrogant and self-absorbed. She also has no affection for the Pack, but I believe her when she says none of her Coven did this."

"You've got to be kidding me," Tegan bit out.

"Look, I know the easy thing to do is to blame the Coven, but after Emma's death and the vampire body at the scene, things just aren't adding up. I think both murders were set up to create conflict between the Pack and the Coven. To instigate a war between your two races." I heaved a sigh. I needed them to believe me, because if they didn't, war was sure to come. I didn't think they would tolerate another unsolved murder within their ranks.

There was a chance I was wrong about this, but my gut was telling me I was on the right track, and it rarely led me astray. I had to at least try.

"Is anyone here familiar with psykers?" I asked.

"What the hell is a psyker?" Mauro asked in a deep baritone voice.

"A psyker is a human with psychokinetic abilities. Essentially, they have psychic powers. Some can read minds, others can teleport, and some hold power over the elements. A psyker is still human. They live an average human lifespan and don't have any regenerative abilities like shifters or vampires outside of healing at an accelerated rate, but psykers are not easy to kill. And most can take you down before you ever get close." I paused to let my words sink in. "There is an organization called PsyShade, and it recruits psykers, conditioning them to view both the Pack and the Coven as abominations, along with every other paranormal species."

The information Twitch had dug up was a gold mine filled with more psyker and PsyShade knowledge than I could have imagined. I still felt somewhat in the dark and like I should have known most of this already. But I was satisfied that I had a good handle on it now. I'd spent all night going over every note and reference Mike had given me.

"Their goal is to restore the world order by reinstating a human-led government and eliminating anyone who they've deemed a threat. The Packs are an obvious threat, and since the Pacific Northwest Pack is the largest in the US, what I've been able to piece together is that if you fall, the other packs will submit rather than risk the same casualties. They don't just want a war. They want to exterminate you."

When I finished, the entire room erupted into chaos. There were growls and snarls. Everyone spoke over one another, and many called me a liar. Declan sat back in his chair and watched as pandemonium ensued.

After two minutes had passed, he'd finally had enough. He stood with an eerie calm and let loose a vicious roar. The hairs on the back of my neck stood on end, and I had to fight my instinct to crawl under the table and hide. He was one scary bastard.

Instantly, the room became quiet, and all eyes zeroed in on Declan.

"Aria, would you please share proof with our council of the existence of the psykers?" he asked. Beneath the table, James squeezed my hand, and I squeezed back before rising from my seat. James stood as well, pulling the chair out for me. I stepped around it and positioned myself at the opposite end of the table to give everyone a clear view.

I hadn't wanted to do this part. I'd argued with James for nearly an hour, but I couldn't see a way out of it. Not if the Pack was going to believe me.

I was ready though. If shit hit the fan, I had a bag packed and ready and could hightail it out of town within the hour.

I held my arms slightly out before me, palms facing up. Closing my eyes, I pulled from deep inside of me, directing my energy towards my outstretched hands. In seconds, the temperature in the room began to rise. Seconds after that, flames encompassed my hands. I focused as hard as possible on keeping the flames large enough for everyone to take notice, but not so large that they'd overwhelm me.

Fire had a way of consuming. It called to you, a silent chant to let it grow and run free.

Hearing audible gasps, I opened my eyes and gauged their expressions. The twins had narrowed eyes, their gazes assessing. Jessica and Mauro seemed unperturbed, as if they'd already known. Eva looked angry. Yvonne was biting her lip, looking concerned. And Robert—Robert had that same feral grin on his face, like he'd just found a tasty snack.

With all eyes still on me, I allowed the flames to lick up my arms. The flames pushed farther and soon encompassed my entire body, even hiding my face. After a full minute, I called my fire back inside of me.

It took longer than I'd have liked, but after a slight internal struggle, I was able to release a sigh as the pressure eased. I'd been practicing my control, but even that small demonstration took its toll. An itch remained under my skin.

"Thank you for the demonstration," Declan said, completely unfazed. He knew what I could do. James had shared the information with him before I'd arrived. He'd never seen it before, yet he acted like a woman bursting into flames was an everyday occurrence.

When I sat again, Robert leaned into me. "That was wicked, and hot," he said, placing his hand on my forearm. "Shit!" he yelped, recoiling.

He stared down at his palm, burned and covered in blisters. His eyes shot from his hand to me, a look of shock on his face.

I shrugged my shoulders and offered him a small smile.

My bad.

Not.

He would heal in minutes. It was nothing to get upset over. The Lyc-V in his system was already repairing the damage, and soon his hand would be unblemished, no signs of any burn. Too bad.

Declan cleared his throat. "As I was saying. We have a new threat. One we have never faced before, and we need to prepare ourselves."

Chapter Eighteen

I walked across the parking lot of Sanborn Place while Jennifer waited in the car. After my demonstration, Declan had requested that she accompany me back to the office to touch base with Mike. He had called earlier and left a message saying he'd found more information and to come by the office when I was finished at the Compound.

I walked into the building and froze at the threshold. The thick scent of blood assailed my senses. I wrinkled my nose and quickly scanned the room—nothing out of place—but I knew something was wrong. Careful not to make any unnecessary sounds, I slowly crept into the office and let my nose guide me through the darkened room to the metallic scent.

I didn't have shifter senses, but the scent was so strong.

My heart hammered in my chest. No. No. No. Worry coiled tight in my stomach.

As I stalked through the room, the offensive smell grew stronger. I turned the corner and saw a pair of legs stretched out on the floor, barely visible behind the bulk of a desk. Thick legs, encased in grey slacks. Shoes, well-worn leather but polished to a shine. The exact shoes that Mike wore to the office every day.

A chill of dread settled deep in the pit of my stomach as I inched closer, tears already forming in the corners of my eyes. Moving completely around the desk, I found Mike's body splayed on the ground, a shaking hand clutched to his stomach.

I rushed to his side and pressed my hand to his wound. I couldn't stop the blood from seeping through my fingers. It was warm and thick. Panic filled me.

"Mike—oh God! Mike, what happened?" I pressed my hand more firmly against his stomach. Blood was rapidly pooling all around me. The logical side of my brain knew he was losing too much, knew that he was beyond saving, but I couldn't give up on him.

"A … Ar … Ari … you need …"

"Shh …it's okay. We're going to get you some help. Everything is going to be okay." I blinked several times in an effort to keep my emotions in check, but it was no use. Tears leaked from the corners of my eyes against my wishes and fell down my cheeks.

"JENNIFER!" I screamed, hoping she could hear me outside. I prayed that her shifter senses would pick up on the sound. I couldn't leave Mike's side to run for help. He wouldn't make it. If I let go of his stomach, he'd bleed out in a matter of seconds.

"JENNIFER!" I screamed again. My voice grew hoarse as I struggled to contain my sobs.

"It's going to be okay. Just hang on, all right? I promise, just please, please hang on." I was babbling, not knowing what to say or if I was saying it aloud for his benefit or my own. I needed to believe it would be okay. I couldn't lose him. I just couldn't.

His breathing grew wet and labored, and as I continued to hold my hand to his wound, I watched as his eyes dimmed, his body giving up the fight.

"No, no, no, don't you leave me," I shouted, shaking him awake. His eyes fluttered open, and when his gaze met mine, he smiled. I tried to smile back but could barely hold back the sobs clogging my throat.

Mike lifted his blood-coated hand and cupped my cheek. His hand shook from the effort.

"Aria, my sweet Aria."

"Shh … don't talk."

Mike shook his head. A tear leaked from the corner of his eye.

Distantly, I heard the office door open and quick footsteps headed in our direction.

"Run," Mike wheezed out. "They came for you, not me. Run."

"What are you talking about?" I asked him as Jennifer came up behind me. She had the first aid kit with her. The one I kept in the trunk for emergencies, but she didn't bother opening it. She knew it was too late, just as I did, but I still wanted to try. I had to. I owed it to Mike to at least try.

I removed one of my hands from Mike's stomach and hastily opened the first aid kit before rifling through its contents. Grabbing gauze and tape I tried to staunch the flow of blood, but it just kept seeping through.

I pulled Mike's shirt up and realized why. What I'd assumed was a stab wound to his stomach, was more. Mike had four separate entry points that I could see, each one bleeding heavily.

"Oh, God."

"You can't fix that," Jennifer whispered to me. A restraining hand on my shoulder.

I shook her off. "Yes, I can. I have to." I sniffed and wiped at my eyes with the back of my hand. I could do this. We would fix it. There had to be a way.

I moved to look for more gauze. We were going to need a lot more gauze.

There wasn't any more, and I needed more. "I need more gauze," I told her.

She put her hands over mine, stopping my movements. "Aria, he's gone."

I looked up. "What are you talking about?" I shook my head in disbelief.

"Aria, look. I can barely hear his heartbeat anymore. His breathing is lessening. Let him go."

"No, I can't!" I dropped everything and reached for his face. "Mike? Mike! Please, please wake up." I chanted it over and over again. "Please, just wake up. Please." My vision blurred. I could barely see through my tears. A sob finally broke loose, and I crumpled over him. "Please, don't leave me," I begged, clutching his body to mine.

I turned to Jennifer. "You have to do something."

"There isn't any—"

"Yes, there is," I said, cutting her off. "Turn him."

Her eyes widened. "I can't."

"You can. There isn't anything stopping you. Please," I pleaded.

She shook her head. "You don't know if it's what he would have wanted. And even if I try, there's no guarantee it would work. He's lost too much blood."

"I don't care. Just try. Please. Just try."

She nodded and reached down toward Mike. Before her hand touched him, though, his chest stopped moving, and his breathing ceased completely.

Mike's blood continued to pool around me. Distantly I wondered how any one person could have so much blood inside of them. I felt like I was swimming in it.

I didn't care that his blood coated my hands or that I had streaks of it across my face. My chest ached. I felt physically ill, but not from the blood. No. This was different. I felt weak, my body worn. There was a gaping hole in my chest now that I didn't think could ever be filled. My head was spinning over the loss. "Oh, God. Marian!" How was I going to explain this?

Jennifer was talking, her hands on my shoulders. But I had no idea what she was saying. It all felt so far away. It didn't matter anyway. Nothing mattered anymore. Mike was gone. He was really gone. She couldn't turn him now. Not without a heartbeat, without a pulse.

My heart plummeted into my stomach, and suddenly I felt cold, but only briefly, before numbness set in.

I flashed back to the day I'd found Daniel, the pool of blood, the loss …

Jennifer was shaking me now, hard. I wanted her to stop. Why wouldn't she just leave me alone? I just wanted to be alone.

Frustrated that she couldn't see that, I finally sat up, glaring at her through my tears as flames began licking my fingers.

"Get off of me."

Our eyes locked for a moment before she suddenly froze. Her head turned towards the office entrance, and she rose slowly to her feet.

"We need to go," she clipped out, eyes hard.

I shook my head. I wasn't going anywhere. She could go, but I was staying. I wasn't going to leave Mike alone.

Jennifer crouched down in front of me, her hands on my shoulders again, ignoring the flames rising over my arms and shoulders. She winced in pain, but her eyes bored into mine, demanding my attention.

"Aria. I need you to look at me. Okay? Focus. He's gone, but there are several vampires outside right now. I can smell them. We need to go. Now!"

"I … I can't." I looked back down at Mike. "I can't leave him like this."

She grabbed my chin and forced my gaze back to hers. "You have to," she said through gritted teeth before she pulled me up with her from the floor.

I didn't want to be touched. Who the hell did she think she

was? Anger rushed through me like a vicious flood, and I jerked free from her grip once more.

"Don't touch me."

"Aria, before Mike died, he said they were here for you. He told you to run. We need to do that now. I need you to run. I can take on a vampire. I can even take on two of them, but any more than that, and I might lose. We might lose." The last was said louder.

Faintly, I remembered Mike's final words.

"Is there a back entrance?"

Before I could respond, she started pulling me away, and blindly I followed, unable to stir up the will to fight her anymore.

As we reached the back door, I heard glass shatter.

"Shit," Jennifer said under her breath. She pulled me closer.

"Come on, I know she's around here somewhere," an unfamiliar voice said.

"Dumb bitch. We'll see how she feels when we do to her what Ryan here did to that old man."

Two men laughed in unison. "Old bastard. He didn't even put up much of a fight," another voice said.

I saw red. These were the vampires responsible for Mike's death. They were the ones that took him away from me. Without thought, I walked towards the voices. Jennifer reached out for me but quickly drew back when her hand made contact, the heat from my skin causing a visible burn.

My fire had grown and turned from an orange glow to a bright hot white, coating my skin from head to toe in a thin layer of flames.

"Shh … I heard something," one of the men said, the one who had spoken first.

Taking several more steps, I turned the corner that hid them from my view. I felt more than heard Jennifer approach from behind, but she kept herself hidden. She probably thought she was going to back me up. I didn't need any backup, though. These men killed Mike. They'd all die by my hand.

Three vampires stood before me, all in similar attire—dark clothing, long leather trench coats. God, couldn't they at least be original? They were all Spike wannabes, and a small part of me found that comical in a morbid way.

"Well, look what we have here," one of the vamps said. "Wanna play?" A wide grin spread across his face, making his wickedly sharp fangs all the more visible.

Idiot. I was going to make them burn.

"You killed my friend." My voice sounded cold even to my own ears.

The second vamp made a sad face. "Aww, are you upset, little girl?" A sadistic smile quickly replaced his frown. "Your friend didn't put up much of a challenge. You'll make this interesting for us, though, won't you?" The bastard laughed, the other two joining in. "We've got a score to settle with you, and your little party tricks aren't going to be any help."

Distantly I wondered what score he was talking about, but I didn't really care. They'd killed Mike. That was enough for me to condemn them all. I wasn't usually the blood thirsty type. But for them, I'd make an exception. The party trick comment had me grinning.

They didn't realize my flames were real. I'd show them.

Without another word, I threw my head back and opened my arms wide. I'd always worked hard to keep a leash on my abilities. Never trusting myself, never knowing just how much power I had within me.

I didn't hold back this time. I let all of my anger and grief rise to the surface, and before the suckheads could so much as blink, I let it all go.

I focused on the two vampires closest to me. The room flashed in a wave of blinding light. The fire so hot that for a brief moment, it shone blue. Within seconds, two of the vamps were incinerated, along with the majority of the surrounding furniture. The charred smell of burning wood wafted through the room.

The third looked horrified. I'd saved him for last. He was the one the others referred to as Ryan. He was the one who'd killed Mike.

I drew my daggers from my waist, a thin white flame covering the steel edge.

"Wha ..."

"You killed my friend," I said in a deadpan voice. "So, I killed yours."

He backed up two paces, arms held out in front of him in a sign of surrender.

"Look, I don't know what you are, but—"

I cut him off. "Stop talking."

Taking a deep breath, I called my fire back inside of me so it no longer covered my body. It took significant effort, but I was determined. I wanted this to last.

As soon as the flames receded, Ryan attacked. Exactly as I'd expected.

His speed gave him an advantage, but my rage fueled me. A blur moved to my right, and I slashed out my blade, drawing a line across pale flesh. Ryan paused, bringing a hand to his cheek and drawing a finger along a thin line of blood.

I smiled. There was a reason daggers were my weapon of choice. They were intimate. They required you to get up close and personal with your opponent. To see every nick and slice you issued. A sword required too much distance for my liking. No, I wanted to look into this bastard's eyes as I carved his heart from his chest.

I didn't believe in murder. But I sure as hell believed in justice.

Ryan's lip curled. Without thought, I struck, both blades connecting with the flesh below his shoulders. I pushed with all my might, ramming him into the back wall. He snapped his teeth, like a vicious animal, barely missing my face.

With another push, I buried my daggers through flesh and into plaster. I stared into his cold eyes, an amber glow illuminating them, and relished the grimace on his face as I gave each dagger a brutal twist.

"Why are you targeting me?" I asked.

He laughed, a grating sound that chafed my senses.

"Your interference will be your demise," he spat out.

So much for getting a real answer. Before he could jerk free from my hold, I pushed my fire out in a concentrated effort, directing the flame to the daggers embedded within him. His eyes grew wide as his body burned from the inside out. Smoke furled from his ears, nose, and mouth.

I'd never seen a vampire die that way, but I watched that amber glow in his gaze dim as his undead flesh grew dry, then crisp, falling in an ashy rain all around me.

It only lasted a moment before my head began spinning, the release of energy so great that I struggled to keep my eyes open. I jerked my blades free from the plaster, small wisps of ash floating away from the crumbling corpse in the invisible breeze.

I swayed on my feet and looked around at the three distinct piles of ash. A satisfied smile tugged at my lips. And then, my world pitched on its end, and it all went black.

Chapter Nineteen

I woke up with a pounding headache. It was becoming my new normal. A wave of nausea caught me off guard when I tried to sit up. I collapsed back against the cushioned surface behind me with a groan and curled into myself.

"Don't try to get up yet, or you'll be throwing up all over the place and mmm ... mm, Annabeth Maple does not clean up vomit, no she does not."

The voice was unfamiliar, but I recognized the heavy accent. The woman sounded as if she had just stepped off a plane from Georgia. Not that I'd ever been before, but, well, I knew a southern accent when I heard one.

She bustled over to my side, helping me into a seated position before bustling to a nearby counter.

"You'd best start looking after yourself. That poor boy! When he saw Jennifer bring you to me ..." She was shaking her head now. "The look on his face, like he'd seen a ghost. The Hunter, he don't scare easy, but you, missy, you gave him quite the fright. Look at you," She waved a tongue depressor at me. "You're all skin and bones. Don't you ever eat?"

Walking back towards me, she placed a meaty hand on her floral fabric-covered hip. "Well?" she asked.

I frowned at her. "Yes, I eat." Why did I feel like a small child being scolded?

"Mmhmmm … sure, you do. That's why you passed out like you did. Open up," she said, holding the depressor out in front of my face.

"Who the hell are you?" I tried for commanding, but instead, my voice came out scratchy and weak.

"Don't you take that tone with me, young lady." She wagged her finger at me. "I am Miss Maple, and I'm responsible for looking after you. James entrusted you to me, so don't make me regret agreeing to help the poor boy out. Now, open up."

I did as she asked, unsure what to say. If James trusted her, then she wasn't a threat. At least I didn't think she was. She did a quick check of my throat, then tossed the stick in a nearby waste bin.

"You need to eat more. If you did, you wouldn't be passing out all willy-nilly. Our girls, they eat. That's how they have the energy to shift, and you obviously didn't have enough juice to do whatever it was you did last night."

"What are you talking about?" My stomach still rolled with every movement I made.

She stopped before me. "Don't you remember?"

I thought about it for a moment, and like a crashing wave, it all hit me. Mike was gone.

My vision blurred with tears as I watched Annabeth walk to the door, open it, and poke her head out. She said something in a hushed tone that I couldn't make out before coming back in.

My breath hitched and my hands began to shake.

Annabeth busied herself for several minutes, her back to me as she stood once more in front of the nearby counter. I ignored her and stared at my hands, remembering last night's events.

Vampires had come for me, but instead found Mike. I replayed his death in my mind.

There had been so much blood. Looking down at my hands, I saw they were now clean. All signs of Mike's blood were gone, but the sensation lingered on my skin. The metallic tang of it filled my nose as I recalled how it had dripped from my fingers and coated my arms. I struggled to keep the contents of my stomach down.

The door opened, and in walked James with Jennifer close behind. James's hair was tousled as if he'd just woken up. His eyes were rimmed red, and he looked ill. A slight green tinged his complexion. He walked over to my side, an air of caution in his every step.

I felt a tear escape and make its way down my cheek. Just seeing him tore the hole in my chest wider. Mike was gone. James was all I had left.

James paused beside me, but just stood there, his hands awkwardly in his pockets. Jennifer hung back a bit. I turned my gaze to her, and she blanched. I was pretty sure if I had shifter senses, I'd smell fear on her. I couldn't blame her after what I'd done last night.

I turned my attention back to James. "He's gone," I choked out.

James nodded.

I wrapped my arms around my legs and made myself as small as possible as tremors racked my body. My tears flowed freely, and for the first time in years, I broke down and sobbed without caring who saw me. My eyes flooded with moisture, and my lungs heaved in an effort to take in breaths between my broken cries. I felt empty.

The loss of my parents had been painful, but this—I couldn't handle it.

The tremors quickly turned into shakes, and the cold, empty

feeling was replaced by an overwhelming heat. My tears began to sizzle on my cheeks, the moisture quickly evaporating.

"She's going to do it again," I heard Jennifer say. Panic in her voice.

Waves of heat akin to those you see on asphalt on a hot summer day rose from my arms, but I didn't care.

"Ari?" James said cautiously. His voice made my grief that much worse. He must think I was a real freak show now. He wouldn't even get close to me.

"Aria. You need to calm down." His voice sounded far away now. Distant and easily ignored.

"What's happening?" I faintly heard Annabeth ask.

"Nothing, she just needs some space. Clear the room," James ordered.

There were sounds of retreating footsteps before I felt a dip in the mattress.

"Aria, look at me," James said.

I shook my head. Grief consumed me as I felt myself spiraling.

"Aria, please. I know Mike is gone, but I'm here, okay? I'm right here." He rested his hand on my shoulder. The smell of burning flesh instantly hit my senses. I jerked away from his touch, horrified to see smoke wafting from his hand.

"I'm so sorry."

"Hey, shhh … It's okay. I'm okay. Just call your fire back for me. Can you do that?"

I looked down at my hands. Small flames climbed along my fingers. I clenched my eyes shut and tried to concentrate. Seconds passed, turning into minutes, and nothing changed.

"I can't."

"Yes, you can. Focus. You can do this."

I tried again. I sucked in a deep breath as the flames slowly dwindled all around me. My body worked to absorb the flames, taking them back inside by sheer force of will. When the last of the flames had retreated, James jerked me into his embrace, and I buried my face in his shoulder.

"It's okay," he told me. "Everything is going to be okay."

My body was still overheated, and I worried the contact with me would still burn him, so I pulled away.

"I've got you," he reached for me again.

"Don't. I don't want to hurt you." My voice was barely above a whisper, cracking with nearly each word.

"Ari, I'm a wolf. Super healing abilities remember?"

I nodded, thankful for small victories but still consumed by my grief. I knew I should pull away.

"I want to go home," I whispered.

"Soon, okay? I'll take you home soon."

I nodded and allowed him to ease me back into the bed. He kept his hand on mine, the touch giving me a small piece of security. I lay there for what felt like hours while he ran his fingers over my hair and held my hand. I was grateful that shock had taken over. It served to cushion my heart, at least for a little while.

The door opened, and I heard someone enter the room. I pulled myself back into a sitting position, my arms shaking from the effort.

"Ms. Naveed. I'm very sorry for your loss." Declan Valkenaar stood at the edge of my bed dressed in jeans and a navy T-shirt that hugged the cut ridges of his abdomen.

I flicked a glance towards him. His words seemed sincere, but something in his tone put me on edge. "Thank you." I pushed my hands against the bed to sit up straighter. "I appreciate your help, but I think I should go home now."

Declan gazed at me through hooded eyes, a small frown marring his striking features. His bright emerald eyes took on a metallic quality, and I knew his beast was near the surface.

He moved closer to the bed, stalking forward. A definite feline grace to his gate. "Ms. Naveed, I think it best if you stay here within the Compound while you recover, and we investigate further into those responsible for the death of your friend and the attack on your life."

"I appreciate your concern," I told him. "I really do, but I'm not Pack. I don't belong here." Out of the corner of my eye, I saw James stiffen.

Declan clenched his jaw. "Regardless, we think it best that you stay."

I wiped my face and narrowed my eyes, my gaze traveling from him to James and then back. James avoided my scrutiny, guilt written all over his face. Declan, however, looked determined. I had a feeling that staying within the Compound wasn't a request. It was an order.

"Look, I appreciate your concern, but I'm going home."

A firm hand rested on my shoulder, effectively stopping me from rising. I turned my head, focused a scowl on that hand, then let my gaze travel up to Declan's stern face. "You have no authority over me."

"That may be true, but my request for you to stay comes from our concern for your safety and wellbeing. You are in no condition to be alone right now."

"And you're the judge of that?" I scoffed.

"I'll look after her," James said.

Declan growled, and James looked away. I shook my head. I didn't need a babysitter. I was a grown woman, for Christ's sake.

"Aria."

It was the first time Declan had used my first name. I glared at him, suspicion warring with exhaustion.

"Please. Just for a few days. Allow us to look after you. Once we're assured your life is no longer in danger, you can return to your apartment. This is just a precaution."

James remained silent during our exchange, but his expression showed genuine concern.

"Fine," I conceded. When I'd regained my strength, I knew I'd regret this, but for now, I didn't have the energy to argue.

"Good. James will show you to the room you'll be staying in. Get some rest. We'll discuss last night's events in the coming days when you feel up to it."

I nodded and watched as he left the room.

James returned to sit next to me and grasped my hand. "Thank you."

"For what?"

"For being reasonable."

I nodded, unable to muster up a better response. Though when I could, he was going to get a piece of my mind.

"I'm going to pick you up okay?" He looked hesitant, like I might bite off his head.

Inwardly, I smiled, because under normal circumstances, I totally would. "I can walk."

"No, you can't. Just be quiet, and let me look after you."

I frowned but wrapped my arms around his neck when he scooped me into his embrace. I rested my head on his shoulder, the steady thrum of his heartbeat comforting.

I must have dozed off.

My eyes briefly fluttered open when I felt James lower me onto a plush mattress. He pulled a comforter over me. "I'll be back to check on you later. Get some rest."

Letting out a muffled sigh, I closed my eyes and listened to James's retreating footsteps.

Chapter Twenty

I stood on the roof of the Pack Compound and stared at the never-ending tree line and lush foliage that covered the vast acreage owned by the Pack. I could faintly make out a scattering of small cottages around the grounds. Pack homes, for those who wanted more privacy than what the main building allowed but still wanted to remain under Pack protection.

"I don't like this." Inarus tilted his head to the side as he listened to the crack of lightning that echoed around us. He'd teleported onto the roof when I went out for some alone time.

Had I been in my right frame of mind, I would have been shocked by the display of his abilities. I hadn't known he could teleport, but at this moment, I didn't particularly care what he could do. I wasn't quite sure why he had come or how I felt about him being here, but my mind wasn't ready to deal with that.

The loss of Mike still had me reeling, and the knowledge that my mother was alive was more than I was able to take in.

I took in a deep breath, anticipating the coming rain with a sense of peace. I wasn't sure what to say to him. There was so much distrust between us now, and I didn't know how to bring it up. I wasn't even sure if he was aware of the doubt that filled me.

"It'll be okay." I'd already told him about the attack at Sanborn Place. It was the only explanation I had for why I was now staying at the Compound. For the time being, at least. "I'll get some rest, call Rebecka to sort everything out, and then I can go home. And everything can all go back to normal."

"Is that what you want?" he asked.

I stared at him and shrugged. "Yes. Of course. Why wouldn't it be?"

"It's just ..." Inarus paused and twisted the ring on his right index finger.

"What?"

"Why did you leave me the other night? Did I upset you somehow?"

I shook my head. "I got a message from Mike. That's why I was at Sanborn Place ..." My words trailed off. Why bother lying?

I slumped my shoulders and stared down at my black leather boots.

"Aria, I saw the look on your face when you turned away. You looked like you'd seen a ghost. What happened?"

"It's nothing, really. Please, just drop it." A part of me wondered if he knew. Another part thought he did and that he was toying with me. In the end, did it really matter?

Inarus studied me, and I avoided his gaze, afraid he'd see right through me.

"You should go inside," he said abruptly. "A storm's moving in, and you probably need to rest." He moved to place a comforting hand on the small of my back, but I pulled away.

"The rain is exactly what I need."

Inarus looked at me quizzically. "You enjoy the rain?" A slight frown marred his features and his grey-blue eyes darted toward the skies.

I nodded in confirmation. The rain was one of the reasons I'd come to Spokane. Rain was a way of cleansing the earth. Of washing away the dirt and grime, and it reminded me of new beginnings. Rain made me feel at peace, despite the fact that it seemed so opposing to my natural pyrokinetic abilities.

It didn't rain in Spokane nearly as much as it did in Seattle, but for me, it was just the right amount. After everything that had happened over the past few days, a cleansing was exactly what I needed. I wanted to just let it all go, clear my head and feel something other than pain or grief.

"I love the rain," I told him honestly.

His frown grew deeper. I laughed out loud at his expression, ignoring the ache in my chest. My laugh sounded forced, even to my own ears, but I needed this as if it were the very air I breathed. I tugged his arm and led him farther into the wide-open space. A slight drizzle began, and I knew it would turn into a heavier rain any moment.

Inarus squinted his eyes to keep the moisture at bay, and once I released his hand, he shoved both hands deep into his pockets.

"How can you enjoy this? You're getting wet, and soon you'll be soaked. This rain will become miserable."

I turned towards him. "You have to feel the rain. Embrace it, and you'll experience more than just the wet."

I could tell that he didn't get it but smiled anyway when the second strike of lightning splintered the sky and the rain turned into a torrential downpour. Walking to the middle of the roof, I spread my arms wide and turned in a slow circle, my face tilted upward.

I let the rain pour down my face, invigorated by each droplet that fell against my skin. In a way, the earth was crying for me over Mike's death. I still felt like crying, but I'd already broken down once. I wouldn't again. Not until I brought those responsible to justice.

Vampires had killed him, and someone had been pulling the strings behind the three I'd killed. I still didn't know who was behind Daniel's death. Nor did I know who was behind Emma's, though I had my suspicions. But I did know who was responsible for Mike's. Their deaths had come too quickly. I should have made them suffer more, drawn out their agony. But there were others. The vampires responsible had gotten their orders from someone higher up. I would find out who, and I'd make them pay.

"Aria," Inarus called. I turned toward him. "Get out of the rain." He waved me toward him.

I shook my head and continued to spin until I was dizzy. I felt myself teetering on the edge of balance, and when my boot slipped against the slick surface, I threw my arms down to catch myself. But he was there, and instead of landing on the cold, wet pavement, I found myself in Inarus's arms.

He was crouched down with my body tucked gently in his arms. I looked up into his crystal clear, grey-blue eyes, and my breath caught at the look of longing in his gaze. He gently tucked a wet tendril of hair behind my ear, his eyes never leaving mine.

"I believe," he began, "that this rain you're so fond of, may be growing on me."

I felt a tentative grin begin at his admission and reached up to cup the side of his face. I didn't know why I was allowing the contact. I didn't trust him. He was likely the enemy. I needed to be on guard around him, not swooning over his proximity.

I held my body perfectly still as he slowly lowered his face to mine, giving me every opportunity to pull away, but I didn't. Couldn't. I needed to feel something good. Something that would make all of the pain go away.

When his lips gently brushed mine, fire burned deep in my veins and sweat dripped down my back despite the chill of the cold night air and cool rain. His lips were so soft. I melted into the contact.

When he pulled back, I saw the reflection of lightning in his eyes. I reached up and touched my bottom lip. Remnants of his kiss ghosted along my senses.

Abruptly, Inarus stood up, pulling me with him. Once I regained my balance, he released me and quickly stepped away, distancing himself, and refusing to make eye contact with me.

I shook it off and turned away, suddenly feeling awkward and embarrassed. Hands tucked in my jacket pockets, I made my way towards the door that led to the stairwell that would take me back within the Compound. I didn't bother to look back.

God, how could I be so stupid? So naïve?

"Aria …" Inarus called my name as I reached for the door handle. I stopped for a second, waiting to see if he would continue, but when all I heard were the sounds of rain splashing against the concrete and thunder in the skies, I went inside.

I didn't need this. I had enough going on in my life. I didn't know why I felt rejected or why suddenly the ache in my chest was more painful than it had been moments ago. I barely knew him. He was nothing to me.

So, why did it hurt?

I WAS SOAKED TO THE BONE AS I MADE MY WAY BACK downstairs, frustrated beyond reason. Stupid! That was so incredibly stupid. I was furious with myself for allowing the touch. For allowing him to get under my skin. I gave him power over me that I never gave to anyone.

I stormed down the stairs, berating myself and cursing my ignorance as I made my way to the room where Declan had insisted I stay. When I found it, I threw the door open and stomped in, coming face to face with James. I paused just inside the threshold, my hand still on the doorknob. James looked up from where he sat on the side of the bed.

"Hey," he said.

"Hi."

Neither of us said anything else for several moments, and I

started to get the sinking feeling that I was in trouble.

James ran his hands through his hair, exhaling a sigh.

"Look, I know you need to rest but, can we talk?"

I nodded and made my way into the room. The door closed behind me with a snick that sounded loud to my ears. I kicked off my boots and grabbed a towel from the nearby dresser, drying my hair as I sat across from James in a wicker chair.

"What did you want to talk about?" I asked, leaning forward in my seat.

James exhaled a breath and looked around the room before meeting my gaze. "It's about Inarus."

I eyed him warily. I wasn't sure, yet, if Inarus was friend or foe, though I'd prefer him to be a friend, despite our awkward moment. James also didn't know that he'd teleported his way onto the Compound roof.

I felt slightly traitorous for not telling him. I wondered if I should. Maybe the Compound's security wasn't as solid as they believed it to be.

I nodded for James to continue.

"I had his placed searched."

My mouth dropped open. Part of me was upset on Inarus's behalf for the invasion of privacy, but another part wondered what James had found. Whatever it was, the grim expression on his face right now meant that it wasn't good.

"He isn't who he says he is."

Well, I knew that already. "Care to elaborate?"

James reached inside his pocket, pulled out an envelope, and handed it to me. Inside were several photographs of me taken during the last few weeks. "He's been watching me? Spying on me?" My stomach dropped. I rifled through the photographs, disturbed by such a violation of my privacy. "He was following me? Bastard!"

James nodded his head and then handed me what looked like a small cell phone. I lifted my brows in question.

"It's a burner phone. One of our younger Pack members found it in his room. Check the message log."

I began scrolling through a series of text messages, all belonging to a single conversation.

Unknown: Status report

Inarus: Pack is blaming the Coven as planned. Phase 2 is moving into place.

I scrolled farther down the screen.

Inarus: Girl may be a possible asset. I plan to bring her in upon mission completion.

Unknown: Good

My hand began to shake. He had to be talking about me. He planned on taking me to them?

Unknown: Status report

Inarus: Everything is going as planned. No new updates.

Oh, God. I felt sick. How could I have allowed him to play me? "Sonovabitch. When I got my hands on him I—"

James cleared his throat. "Ari—"

"We need to do something!" I stood and began pacing the room. I took several deep breaths, and pushed the fire deeper inside of me.

"The Pack is already moving into place to take him down. I just … I wanted to let you know before we took action."

"I want to be there."

James shook his head. "I don't think that's a good idea."

"He's here."

"What? What do you mean he's here?"

"I mean, he's here. On the Compound. Right before I ran into you, I was talking with him on the roof. He teleported in."

James swore before heading for the door, his movements determined. I grabbed my daggers from the bedside table where I'd placed them earlier and sheathed them in the loops along my belt.

I was going to make Inarus regret ever meeting me.

Chapter Twenty-One

Inarus was right where I'd left him. He stood on the rooftop of the Compound, his back to the door, still dry, despite rain falling around him, a force field of some sort protecting him. Stupid telekinetic abilities. I wanted him to be soaked and cold.

At the sound of our approach, he turned around. James and I were at the front of our party, four shifters whose names I didn't know stood behind as reinforcements.

Inarus's gaze locked with mine, a question evident in his eyes. I glared at him and let him see the full force of my anger.

The Pack mates behind us slowly crept forward when James and I stopped, effectively surrounding Inarus.

"What's this about?" Inarus directed his question at me.

I didn't answer. Instead, I watched as James threw the photographs at him. The images landed in a small puddle near his feet.

Inarus bent to retrieve them and gave them a quick once over before turning his sharp gaze to James. "You searched my place." His statement held more than a hint of accusation. "This isn't what you think."

I didn't let him finish. Shaking my head, I held up the burner phone. "Really? What is, then? Because this right here, it's pretty damning."

His eyes fell. He had to know there was no talking his way out of this.

"That's not mine," he said, the denial rolling off of his tongue easily. Guess he was going to try anyway.

"Shifters can scent a lie," James growled. "And right now, you're lying through your teeth."

Inarus ignored him. "Aria, whatever you found on that phone was planted. It isn't mine. You have to believe me. I would never—"

"No. No more lies. I want the truth. You owe me that much."

Inarus's shoulders slumped in defeat. "I never wanted to hurt you."

I shook my head. This wasn't about me. Inarus was clearly working on the wrong side. "Did you kill Daniel Blackmore?" I kept my voice hard, steady.

He shook his head. "I'd never hurt a child, not even a shifter."

Not even a shifter? My lip curled in disgust.

"And the two girls? Emma and the vampire?" My heartbeat pounded in my ears. Inarus looked away, refusing to meet my gaze. Well, that answered that question. His lack of response was enough of an admission of guilt. I didn't need him to say it aloud to know he was the one responsible.

"Why?" I asked him, my voice laced with steel.

"Aria, you don't understand."

"Then explain it to me!" I shouted. The others took a threatening step closer to Inarus. He barely glanced their way, deciding they weren't a threat. I wasn't surprised. He was a telekinetic. If he wanted to, he could toss them off the rooftop with little more than a thought.

"The shifters shouldn't be in control of this city or any other. Neither should the vampires. Humans should be in control. We aren't the monsters here. They were the ones that ruined everything. They're the reason we don't have a government or a police force. We don't have public education or public hospitals. The HAC is just trying to take back what rightfully belongs to us." His voice took on a menacing quality as he directed his attention to the men surrounding him. "They're an abomination."

"And what about us? What are we? How are we any different?"

"We're human. We aren't monsters or creatures of the night, Aria. We don't massacre cities in a fit of rage or suck blood from innocent people to sustain ourselves."

"No. You just kill innocent children and women without cause," I said in response.

"I didn't kill that boy!" Inarus yelled. His hands fisted at his sides.

"You may not have killed him, but you work for the people responsible for his death, and you did kill Emma and the vampire."

"They're monsters. A freaking bloodsucker and an animal, Aria."

"They were people, Inarus! There were others who cared about them, and you took them away. For what? Because you had orders to do so? That isn't a good enough answer! They didn't deserve to die."

"The vampire was already dead," he shouted. "She didn't deserve to walk this earth any longer. None of their kind do."

"What now?" I asked him.

"Come with me. You don't belong here, with them." He waved his hand at the surrounding shifters.

I shook my head. "I don't want anything to do with the HAC, with PsyShade, or with you." He'd killed Emma. He'd lied to me, played me for information, and all the while he'd planned on turning me in to the very people responsible for murdering a child.

What if he'd had something to do with Mike's death? I knew vampires had killed Mike, but at this point, nothing was beyond Inarus. On top of that, he actually believed in his mission. I could see the unshakable faith in his eyes.

Everyone had taken a hit after the Awakening, but going back to the way things used to be wasn't an option. We needed to adapt, to adjust to our current way of life. We couldn't live in the past or go back to ignoring all things supernatural.

But before I could tell him as much, James spoke up.

"You're going to be taken into custody for crimes against the Pack. When we're done with you, I'm sure the Coven will have more," James said vehemently.

Inarus laughed. "You won't be taking me anywhere."

"You're only going to make things harder on yourself by resisting."

Inarus shook his head. "You don't get it, do you?" He tsked.

I eyed him warily, unsure what he was really capable of.

"I'm a telekinetic. You can't touch me."

James growled, then lunged for Inarus. Between one second and the next, Inarus disappeared, reappearing a few feet from where James stopped.

"Aria," Inarus called from his new position. "Come with me. Let me explain everything. Let me help you understand,"

I shook my head in refusal.

Inarus rubbed the nape of his neck. "Aria, please …" Before he could say anything else, two shifters grabbed him from behind. He disappeared from their grasp, reappearing once again, this time closer, a scant two feet from my position.

I pulled a dagger from my waist, a flame stretching over the blade's surface.

Inarus locked eyes with me. "Are you really going to try and fight me? You know I'm right. You know you don't belong here."

I shook my head. I may not have belonged here, but I certainly didn't belong with him.

Inarus held his hand out to me, his eyes pleading that I take it and go with him.

I shook my head, my eyes hard.

His expression filled with hurt, but it quickly transformed into anger when a dark form sailed through the air, tackling him to the ground. The shifter that attacked rose in the air, lifted by invisible hands and Inarus stared in rage at the man. I looked around to see all of the shifters slowly rising off the ground. Each growling in frustration as they struggled to reach the stone floor beneath them. Only I remained on the ground, Inarus's power directed solely at the shifters surrounding him.

"You're all animals," he cursed. "Worthless." The intent in his eyes was clear. He was going to drop them from the roof. The Pack Compound rose ten stories high. I knew shifters were resilient, but I couldn't chance that they would all survive a fall like that.

Without conscious thought, I threw my blade directly at Inarus's heart. With the wave of a hand, he knocked it away. I drew another and threw it as well. The blade spun in a spiral pattern as it neared its intended target.

Again, he knocked the blade aside. I pulled from within, drawing my fire out. With arms together in front of me, I molded a ball of fire within my hands.

Inarus grinned. "Do you think that will stop me?"

Sweat dripped down my brow from the strain of containing the fire in its shape. When the ball was the size of a basketball, I threw it with everything I had.

As soon as the fireball was free, I lifted the hem of my shirt, reached down to my hip, and ripped my tattooed blade free from my flesh. "Fuck," I muttered out a curse. The pain was excruciating. I'd pulled it out quicker than intended and my skin felt as though it were being flayed from my body.

I threw my final blade at Inarus while he was distracted by

the fire. He deflected the flames, and I saw a triumphant grin on his face right before the tattooed blade pierced his chest.

I was under no illusion that the fire would stop him. But the blade? Yeah. I believed it would do the trick.

The shifters surrounding us dropped to the ground, still within the roof's perimeter. Inarus turned his shocked gaze my way. He looked down at his chest and touched the hilt of the blade with a grimace.

A slow stream of blood dripped from the wound. Inarus ripped the blade free and stared down at it. "How did you …"

"Your powers don't work on it. No magic does. It has mystical properties that make it immune to all others."

He nodded, still in shock. The blade clattered to the ground as he stumbled forward. I fought to remain still. I couldn't run to him. I couldn't help him. He'd made his bed, and now he had to lie in it.

James saw the opportunity and lunged.

But before his fingers could so much as touched a thread of fabric, Inarus disappeared. James caught nothing but air.

We all stood still, waiting for him to pop back in. Seconds became minutes, and we realized he wasn't coming back.

I was relieved this fight was over. But I knew it wasn't the end. War was coming. Whatever Inarus was tied up in, these people would continue their fight for power. They weren't a secret anymore, though. And when they came, I'd be ready.

No one killed innocents in my city.

Chapter Twenty-Two

Declan gave me the okay to head to my apartment and retrieve some of my belongings the next morning. Not that I needed his permission.

I didn't know how long I'd stay at the Compound, but after Inarus's departure, I realized staying with the Pack was probably for the best.

A feline shifter named Hannah accompanied me. She was silent for the most part, offering only one word answers whenever I asked her a question. I didn't mind her silence. It was comforting in a way. Neither of us seemed to feel the need to fill the empty space, and that was all right by me.

Walking into my building, I gave Melody my usual hello then trekked up the four flights of stairs. When I opened my door, Hannah swiftly sidestepped me and entered first.

I rolled my eyes, but followed her in. I stood just inside the doorway as she scanned the room before checking the adjoining rooms. When she gave the all clear, I headed for my bedroom.

I grabbed a backpack from my closet and began stuffing random articles of clothing inside, along with a framed photo I'd kept on my dresser. As I shoved it inside, a faint tapping sound caught my attention.

I turned to the glass door in my bedroom to see Melody perched on the balcony railing, a wide grin on her pretty face. I looked around to make sure Hannah was in the other room, then opened the door and stepped onto the balcony with Mel.

"What are you doing?" I whispered.

She stepped from the railing, and folded her wings in as she rose to her full height in front of me.

"Here." She handed me a folded envelope.

"What's this?" I took the envelope from her hand and ran my finger beneath the seam.

Melody shrugged her shoulders. "A letter, duh. That hunk who lived across the hall from you asked me to deliver it. Normally, I'd say no. I mean, I'm not an errand girl. But then he smiled, and his eyes got all sparkly. He's good … Anyway, I said I'd give it to you, so, here ya go."

"Thanks." I looked up at Mel. "I'm going to be MIA for a while. Can you do me a favor and check in on my place from time to time?" I turned to go back into my apartment.

"Sure thing," she said with way too much pep in her voice.

I stopped and turned back, a glint in my eyes. "Oh and Mel?" I said as she hoisted herself in the air.

"What?"

"Feel free to use and take whatever you'd like. What's mine is yours." I winked and gave her a knowing smirk.

Her smile faded. "You just have to take all the fun out of it. Don't you?"

"Sorry. A girl's got to do what a girl's got to do. But watch the place, and your secret is safe with me. You can rest assured that Ryan will never know."

Her eyes narrowed for a brief moment before she nodded and flew back down to the lower level of the apartment building.

Back inside I sat on my bed and eyed the letter like it was a snake ready to strike. Chiding myself for being afraid of a piece of paper, I unfolded the letter and read what was inside.

> *Aria—*
> *I never meant to hurt you. I have a duty to my people, our people. You have to understand that. You belong with us, with me. I'll give you time, but I can only give you so much.*
> *Until I return,*
>
> *—Inarus*
> *P.S. Your secret is safe with me.*

I STARED AT THE SHORT LETTER, READING IT AGAIN AND again. When Hannah walked into the room, I quickly stuffed it in my back jeans pocket.

"Are you ready?" She lifted a brow.

"Almost. Just give me another minute."

She nodded and headed back out of the room. My heart hammered in my chest and my thoughts went back to the letter. What secret did he mean? Did he know Viola was my mother? It was the only secret I could think of, and I worried what he'd do with the information.

Would he tell her? And how would she react? Maybe she already knew. I couldn't be sure either way.

I stuffed a few last minute items in my pack before zipping it closed. Grabbing it, I headed back into the living room, stopping briefly to retrieve my toothbrush from the bathroom.

"I'm ready," I told Hannah forcing confidence into my voice. But was I ready for what was coming?

I found Declan behind his desk, emerald eyes staring intently at the screen of his computer. I'd walked in without knocking and stood waiting for him to acknowledge my presence.

Tapping my foot impatiently, I saw the slight twitch of his lips before he set his keyboard aside and motioned for me to take a seat. I pulled the masculine wooden chair back and sat down without a word.

Declan leveled me with his hard gaze. His Alpha stare packed a punch, and I had to fight the urge to fidget. I wasn't willing to give even an inch. I wasn't a shifter or a member of his Pack. And I wasn't going to look away just to satisfy his control issues.

After a beat, Declan flashed a smile, showing a hint of fang before leaning back in his chair, hands folded and resting in his lap.

"What can I do for you, Miss Naveed?"

"Aria," I corrected.

Declan inclined his head. "Alright. Aria, what can I do for you?"

"I have a problem."

He waited for me to continue.

I pulled the note from my pocket and slid it across the desk. It was a gamble, but I was going to need allies. Hopefully this show of trust would earn me some points.

Declan studied the note for a moment. A furrow formed between his brows, and his expression hardened. "That is a bit of a problem."

I nodded.

"We assumed we'd be seeing him again. I didn't realize how fixated he was on you. More reason for you to stay here."

"You know what I am. What I can do."

He nodded.

"So, why are you helping me?" I'd done everything in my power to lay low and stay under the Pack's radar. To stay under everyone's radar. Declan had to have an ulterior motive.

He steepled his fingers in front of him. "Miss Naveed, I understand your fear, but you're a trusted friend to my Hunter." He paused. His eyes bore into mine, making sure I understood the weight of that statement. "You are safe here."

"I'm a liability to your Pack." He had to know that.

Declan seemed to weigh his words. "You're right."

My shoulders slumped, and I waited for him to tell me to leave, to grab my things and head out as quickly as possible. Even though I bristled under his authority, I desperately wanted to be accepted. To have the safety and security that the Pack offered.

"I'd still like you to stay, though."

My head shot up at his words, and my mouth hung open. Was he serious?

Declan was somber for a moment. "Aria, there will be a war. I'm nearly certain of it. There is too much bad blood between the vampires and the shifters, and the HAC seems intent on being the spark that ignites the fire. We could use someone with your abilities when that time comes. I know you don't owe any allegiance to the Pack, but I'm hoping that your relationship with James will allow you to consider my offer."

I stared wide-eyed at him. I was an asset? Now I really thought he was crazy.

When I didn't respond, Declan continued. "I'd like to offer you Friend-of-the-Pack status in exchange for your willingness to support our Pack and provide any information possible to help us come out on the winning side of things."

Friend-of-the-Pack status? I wasn't sure what that actually entailed, though I knew it was not offered lightly. The question must have shown on my face, because before I could ask, Declan answered my unspoken question.

He braced his elbows on the edge of the desk, his expression serious. "Friend-of-the-Pack status is not something to be taken lightly. As a Friend-of-the-Pack we offer you our full support and protection in times of need. In addition, we're formally acknowledging our faith and trust in you. You'll have free rein of the Pack grounds and access to all of our resources."

Wow. I wasn't sure what to say. I'd lost a … I didn't know what Inarus was to me, but I'd lost him and somehow gained an ally, and a strong one at that. But …

"What does James think about this?" I asked, my voice hesitant.

Declan paused. "What is your relationship with him?"

I shrugged. "We're friends," I said and looked away from Declan.

"Nothing more?" he pried.

"No. We're just friends."

Declan grunted in acknowledgment. "Will you consider my offer?"

I nodded and stood to leave. "I'll think about it."

"One more thing before you go." Declan handed me back the note, and I shoved it into my jean pocket. "What is the secret he's referring to?"

"The woman, Viola Reynolds," At his nod, I continued, "She's my mother."

Chapter Twenty-Three

I was going to be in so much trouble. I'd told Declan I would consider his offer, and I really would. But I was also taking advantage of it and the freedom it would afford me by sneaking off the Pack's grounds.

Easier said than done.

The Compound was huge, and it had taken me a full hour to locate my car. Sneaking into the Pack's underground parking garage had been surprisingly easy. The hard part would be getting out with my vehicle.

I sidled closer to my car, peering through the darkened lot to ensure that I was still alone. As I reached for the door, a hand landed on my shoulder, causing me to jump with a shout.

Without thinking I pulled a dagger from my waist and twisted to hold it to my attacker's throat.

"What do you think you're doing?" James asked.

Shit. I lowered my blade and shoved him in the shoulder. "You have got to stop sneaking up on me. I could have hurt you."

James flashed me a grin, his white teeth practically glowing in the darkened garage. "Ari?" He ignored my statement, and I chose to ignore the unspoken question.

Instead, I slid into the driver's seat of my car and closed the door.

James leaned into the window, his eyes locked on mine. "Where do you think you're going?"

"Out." I started the engine. The sound of the motor filled the enclosed space. Throwing on my seatbelt, I turned back to James. "Can you move?"

James glowered. He wasn't happy, but I knew he wouldn't stop me. James knew better than most that I refused to be caged. But instead of stepping away and allowing me to leave, he walked around the front of the car, opened the passenger door and climbed in.

"What are you doing?"

"Ari, in less than a week you've been attacked twice. In both instances, you could have died. If you think I'm letting you go off on some harebrained errand on your own, you're crazy."

He had a point. Not that I'd ever admit it aloud.

"Won't Declan be angry at you for letting me leave?"

He shrugged. "I was never ordered to contain you on the Pack grounds."

I nodded as I pulled the vehicle forward and made my escape.

🐾

James wasn't at all happy when I told him where we were going. He was even less pleased when he realized I'd originally planned to go on my own. It couldn't be avoided.

I hadn't made an appointment, and to say that Rebecka was happy to see me would be a gross overstatement.

"What do you want?" she said upon seeing me. At least this time she directed her question at me instead of James.

"I want to know why you sent vampires to attack me at my place of work. Why you're so eager to ignite a war between the Pack and the Coven."

I didn't miss the look of surprise on her face before she masked it. "What are you talking about?"

"I've been attacked by Coven members on two separate occasions, and I want to know why," I said, my voice filled with vehemence.

I left out the bit about Mike's murder. She'd have no sympathies for me, and telling her I'd been hurt by his death would only make me appear weak.

"None in my Coven have done such a thing."

"Liar."

She bared her fangs at me. "Do not presume to lay your blame at my feet."

I bared my teeth at her in a feral sneer. "Your pride and your ignorance will be your downfall."

If she could flush, I imagined she would have done so at that moment. Her eyes blazed crimson in her fury, her face contorting in rage. She appeared to grow in height, standing up straighter and pushing her shoulders back. I glanced over to James to see his eyes locked on Rebecka. Every muscle corded, waiting for the viper to strike.

Despite how dangerous it was to rile up a vampire, let alone one of her age and strength, this was telling. I was starting to believe that maybe she really didn't know what I was talking about.

"I could snap that pretty little neck of yours in a mere second, and then you would be dead, no longer a nuisance. How dare you come to my home and accuse me and my Coven of wrongdoings you have no proof of?"

My anger rose at her threat, and I decided to bring out the big guns. I held my palm out and allowed an orange flame to dance on the palm of my hand.

Her eyes flickered with uncertainty.

"I can light your entire Coven on fire in a matter of seconds. Would you like to find out who's faster?" I challenged.

Her eyes narrowed, but she didn't move. Not that I'd expected her to. She wasn't an idiot. Rebecka was cold and calculating, and I'd just shown all my cards.

Her eyes briefly turned to James, and I could guess her train of thought.

"I've pledged no allegiances," I told her.

James stiffened beside me.

"I'm not interested in your politics. All I care about is stopping this war and finding out why you've been trying to kill me."

I could see the wheels spinning in her mind. "What do you require for your loyalty?"

I shook my head. "I can't be bought, and I'm not taking sides."

"Miss Naveed, I believe you are in fact taking sides right this very moment."

"Will you tell me if it was you that gave the order to have me attacked?"

"I did not."

I flicked a glance to James, but he remained expressionless. I wished he could scent whether she was lying, but vampires didn't experience scent changes under pressure the way a human or shifter did.

"And you still claim to have had no part in Daniel Blackmore's death?"

"I do."

I took a deep breath through my nose. I believed her, which was infuriating. Inarus had already helped to lay Daniel's death at PsyShade's feet. But Mike's death had been at the hand of a vampire. If the order hadn't come from Rebecka, who could it have come from?

"One of yours has ordered an attack on my life twice. I want to know who."

She glared at me but didn't refuse my request. It was more than I could have asked for.

"Look, I'm not here to argue with you. I want answers. I want those responsible for Daniel Blackmore's death. I believe the same group is responsible for the deaths of one of your vampires and a Pack shifter." I watched as something passed over her eyes. Sorrow, perhaps? I shook the notion away. She was a hundreds-of-years-old vampire. One life probably meant nothing to her.

"Someone is trying to draw the Coven and the Pack into a war. I can't let that happen."

"You just claimed you want no part in our politics. What business of it is yours?"

"If you two go to war, we all suffer. All I ask is that you not attack the Pack without just cause. That you ensure you have all the facts before making any rash decisions."

"I never act rashly," she bit out.

"Then we shouldn't have any problems, and there will be no war."

Rebecka smiled, and a shiver ran down my spine.

"I believe we have taken enough of your time." I turned my back to leave, James following behind.

"I will not forget this," Rebecka said as I left.

"Nor will I," I told her. Nor will I.

Nothing was finished. Not with Rebecka, not with Inarus, and certainly not with my mother. But I wasn't giving up. Things were far from over.

Epilogue

Declan

Pacing the confines of my study, irritation bloomed in my chest. Brock stood beside the door, arms folded as he awaited my response.

"We need her," I told him.

Brock nodded but didn't seem convinced. "She isn't Pack."

"I know that," I growled, continuing to pace.

Brock took his job as one of my guards and the head of the Pack's security seriously, but there were instances such as these where I'd rather be alone. Whatever was coming would be big. As Alpha, I needed to ensure that every resource was available to us in the upcoming battle. If we didn't get her on our side, Rebecka would. Or worse, whoever was behind the HAC and PsyShade. She knew little about her own kind. The allure to learn more would be a difficult pull to fight.

"What is her relationship with our Hunter?" I asked. She'd stated they were simply friends, but I'd scented a hint of a lie. Perhaps she wanted there to be more.

"I believe they're friends," was his dull response.

"She claimed the same, but have you seen any hints that their relationship goes beyond friendship?" I asked.

"I don't believe so, sir."

Well, damn.

"Speak with James and find out for certain whether he has feelings for the girl beyond friendship. If he does, tell him it is at his Alpha's request that he pursue them. If he doesn't, find someone else. We need her invested in the Pack. The easiest way to do that is to tie her to one of our own."

"But sir—"

I froze in my tracks and locked my gaze on him. He immediately looked down, eyes on the collar of my shirt. Smart pup.

"I meant no disrespect," he said quickly. "I was only surprised by your suggestion, that one of our own mate with a human woman."

"I said nothing of mating. I would never force one of our people to bind themselves for life to someone they didn't wish to be bound to." No, I would never do that. A mate bond was sacred and something that only happened between shifters.

There were rare instances when a shifter would take a human for a husband or wife but that individual was never their true mate.

My voice rumbled with the hint of growl. My beast was on edge. "I want her enthralled, swooning, taken with one of our men, or women if that is her preference. Find someone who will date the damn woman and wrap her around their damn little pinky. Are we clear?"

"Crystal," he said, turning for the door.

"And Brock?"

He stopped. "Yes, sir?"

"Do it discreetly."

Brock left the room. I sat in the large leather armchair that took up real estate in the corner of my office.

There was something about Miss Naveed that called to the primal beast inside of me. I would need to be careful where she was concerned. She was an asset. Nothing more. I certainly couldn't allow myself to become distracted should she prove to be a threat.

Aria's story continues in
KISSED BY FIRE
Blood & Magic : Book 2
Grab your copy now on Amazon
Turn the page for a sneak peak—

TWENTY-FOUR

Kissed by Fire

Chapter One

I yanked at the hem of the midnight-blue dress I'd borrowed from my neighbor Melody and wondered why the hell I'd decided to wear a dress in the first place.

It was inappropriately short, below freezing outside, and I looked ridiculous.

I didn't do dresses. My wardrobe consisted of steel-toed boots, yoga pants, and t-shirts with inappropriate sayings.

So, why the hell did I let her talk me into wearing this?

I groaned. It was too late to do anything about it now.

The top sported a sweat-heart neckline that refused to stay in place. I wasn't overly busty by any means, I had boobs sure, but I didn't regularly spill out of my clothes and with my everyday clothes I could get by with a sports bra, but the stupid dress was strapless and it kept shifting leaving me feeling exposed despite the well-loved leather jacket I'd thrown over it. And don't even get me started on the bead-work encrusted top. It chafed on the underside of my arms which I was pretty sure were red and raw by now, and when the sun hit it just right, I swear the beads and their jewel like embellishments blinded me.

The whole thing was too much. Too short. Too sparkly. Too ridiculous given the weather.

Wearing anything that belonged to Melody Leis was a bad idea.

"Lesson learned," I muttered to myself and tugged on the hemline, again. Mel's fashion sense was that of a deranged punk-rock pixie. I cringed at the thought of the first dress she'd suggested I wear. It'd been pink, plaid, and pleated. PINK PLAID! How was that not criminal? I would have gone out like a boarding school reject if I'd worn her first suggestion, and you'd think after she'd pulled out that monstrosity, I would've realized her taste in clothes and mine, weren't compatible. But I'd been desperate.

Ugh! Too late to do anything about it now.

I turned away from the biting cold and faced the heavy wooden door. Its scarred surface had once been inviting. Now, the heavy door and protruding iron knocker washed a wave of dread over me.

Deeps breaths. In and out. You could do this.

I chewed on my lower lip.

Nope. I couldn't do this. Coming today had been a mistake and the dress only confirmed it. Marion wouldn't want to see me. She'd probably slam the door in my face.

And could I blame her if she did?

"Of course not." I muttered, worrying the toe of my left high heel into the snow-covered floor mat. If Marion slammed the door in my face, I couldn't and wouldn't blame her. No one wanted to see the woman responsible for their husband's death.

The peach pie in my hands was leaden between my fingers. I could turn tail and run. It wasn't too late. Did it make me a coward? Sure. Did I care …? I was undecided.

The idea of facing Marion made my chest tight and my stomach clench in an uncomfortable knot.

But I owed it to Mike to check in on her. She'd been like a mother to me these past few years. Much as Mike had been my surrogate father. And it was my fault she was a widow now.

Taking a deep breath, I shifted the pie to one hand and lifted the other toward the heavy iron knocker. Winter air swirled around me, raising goosebumps on my bare legs.

Here goes nothing …

The door swung open.

I froze with my hand raised, caught like a deer in headlights. "Shit."

"Nice to see you too, dear." Weariness weighed down her words.

I opened my mouth then closed it. Marion Sanborn's graying hair, normally carefully styled, was pulled into a tight knot at the nape of her neck. Her wire-rimmed glasses rested on the bridge of her nose and did little to hide the dark puffy shadows that told me she'd cried recently.

I hunched my shoulders and stared listlessly down at the pie in my hands. "I …" Dammit. Words weren't coming out.

Marion reached out and tugged me into a warm embrace, the pie awkwardly held between us. "I'm glad you're here." Her vanilla-scented perfume surrounded me in a blanket of comfort. I breathed in the scent and the tight knot in my chest slowly unraveled.

She released me and gave me a quick once over, lifting a single brow when her eyes caught on my heels.

"Too much?" I wobbled for a moment before regaining my balance. The three-inch pumps hadn't been the most practical choice given the current weather or my current occupation— badass mercenary and all—But, Melody insisted I wear heels because of the dress and my closet housed two pairs of worn leather steel-toed boots, a pair of sneakers, and a single pair of flip-flops. None of which would have gone with this outfit, so I'd resigned myself to Melody's heels. I didn't have an alternative.

Though now that I was here, I wished I would have just stuck with the yoga pants and boots. I'm sure I would have been able to find at least one shirt without anything vulgar on it. I had a few solids in the back of my closet.

Marion gave me a small, but warm smile. "It's the middle of winter. Of course, it's too much. Now come inside before you freeze half to death." She turned and motioned for me to follow.

Pressing my heels into the doormat, I tried in vain to get the clumps of snow off before following.

I lingered in the entryway after I closed the door against the bitter cold.

"So … umm …" I stuttered, unable to form words. How did you say, *I'm sorry your husband is dead because of me. I wish it'd been me instead, and I wished I'd killed the bastards responsible more slowly?*

"Hush, dear. Just come have a seat."

When I didn't move, Marion bustled towards me and took the pie from my grasp. She placed it on a nearby table littered with casseroles, pies, plates of cookies, and other baked goods.

I supposed everyone else who'd come to pay their respects had thought food would help, too. I wasn't sure why I'd brought a pie, but it had seemed like the right thing to do. Now I felt like an idiot. Food didn't replace a husband.

Mike's funeral had taken place a little over three weeks ago. Looking at the array of food on the table made me realize just how loved he was. I'd gone to the funeral and watched from a distance, too afraid to face Marion at the time. Too ashamed of the role I'd played in his death. I blamed myself, and rightly so. He'd still be here if it hadn't been for me.

I'd been working a case with the Pacific Northwest Pack. Someone had murdered a seven-year-old boy to incite a war between the shifters and the local vampire Coven. I'd gotten in their way. But when they came for me, they found my boss, Mike, instead.

He'd warned me that the case was too dangerous. I should have listened. Maybe if I had, he'd still be here.

Unable to stand in the entryway any longer, I took a seat on the cream-colored sofa and folded my hands in my lap.

Marion hurried into the nearby kitchen. I heard the refrigerator open and a cupboard door close, and did my best not to fidget while I waited for her return. Anticipation ate at my nerves. Finding a stray fiber on the arm of the sofa, I pulled at the thread, trying to distract myself. For once, my pyrokinesis was silent—no sudden urges to light furniture on fire, which was a relief.

Since Mike's passing, I'd had less control over my abilities than usual. I knew a good part of it was my grief and frustration, but the lack of control was beginning to take its toll. I was glad for once it was staying dormant when I needed it to.

The pungent aroma of coffee filled the air. A few minutes later, Marion emerged from the kitchen carrying two steaming mugs. "Here, dear, drink this."

I gratefully accepted the mug of coffee she handed me, allowing the warmth to seep into my body as I brought the cup up to my mouth and took a tentative sip. Coffee had a way of soothing, and I was grateful that, like me, Marion was a coffee drinker.

I held the mug with both hands and watched Marion over the rim as she took a drink as well. She didn't look angry. Only sad. Her movements were jerky, and her lower lip trembled as she moved to set her cup aside.

If Marion started crying, I didn't know what I would do. I wasn't built to comfort others. I was harsh edges and sharp blades. Not warm and motherly. Not like Marion. My heart clenched at the thought of what she must be going through.

But I had no way to assuage her suffering.

She pulled at the edges of her cardigan, and her gaze wandered to the left side of the room. Photographs lined the living room walls. Mike and Marion's personal hall of fame.

At Sanborn Place—the mercenary guild he'd started from the ground up—Mike had lined the walls with newspaper clippings of cases solved. The moments he was most proud of in his career.

Here, in his home, photographs lined the walls. His proudest moments as a husband. Mike and Marion had no children, but they'd traveled all over the country, and they proudly displayed those memories for guests to see—A photograph of the two of them at the Santa Cruz beach boardwalk. Another in San Antonio, Texas in front of The Alamo.

My gaze landed on their wedding portrait. It hung as the focal point of the room, above the fireplace mantel. They must have been little more than teenagers. Both so young and so in love.

When I returned my attention to Marion, the corners of her mouth lifted into a small smile, though the sadness remained in her eyes.

"We had twenty great years together," she told me.

Moisture pooled in the corners of my eyes and I blinked them away. "I'm so, so sorry." God, wasn't that the truth. Mike and Marion had taken me in when I had no one else. And how had I repaid them? They had deserved better from me.

I rubbed a fisted hand over my chest.

"For what? You didn't take him from me."

I couldn't look up. I fought the emotions threatening to emerge and set my coffee mug aside on the nearby end table.

"It was my fault." I hung my head. "They came for me and killed him instead. He wouldn't have even been there had I not asked him to look into someone for me." The "someone" being Viola Reynolds. The mother I'd long believed dead.

She'd fooled me. Abandoned me at the age of seventeen and left me alone to fend for myself, believing both she and my father died gruesome deaths. My Papa had. But all this time, she'd been alive and well, living under an alias as the leader of the Human Alliance Corporation.

I almost laughed at the irony. I'd found my long-lost mother only to lose my beloved surrogate father.

Marion reached out and clasped my hand in hers. "We knew the dangers of his line of work. Don't carry that guilt with you. It's not your burden. It'll only weigh you down."

I appreciated her words. But I didn't agree with them. Mike's death would follow me no matter where I went. He'd meant too much to me for it not to.

A tear slipped free and slid down my cheek. I hastily wiped it away with the back of my hand.

"Now that you're here, there are some things I'd like to discuss with you."

I nodded, still not bothering to look up as Marion released my hand.

Papers ruffled close by. I sniffed and took a hard swallow, the lump in my throat refusing to go down.

"Mike left Sanborn Place to you," she said without any preamble. "He'd prepared his will last year and named you the beneficiary of both his business and the building in the event of his death."

A flash of surprise coursed through me, and I winced at the mention of the building. Mike died in my arms, and when his attackers returned for me, I'd killed them in a blaze of fury that'd left the office in ruins. I wasn't sure how much of the building survived.

"Why would he leave Sanborn Place to me?" Her words sank in, and the reality of it hit me full force. "Why me? Why not Nico or Taylor?" They were the veteran mercs. The ones with a hell of a lot more experience. I had no idea how to run a business. I was twenty-three. I didn't go to college. Everything I knew was what I learned along the way.

Marion's eyes softened as she handed me a few sheets of paper. My hands shook as I read over each page line by line. Mike named me his sole beneficiary for the business. He'd added my name to the deed on Sanborn Place. It was mine free and clear. Why would he do that?

"Nico and Taylor are great mercenaries. But they were only ever employees. You know he always thought of you as a daughter. The daughter we were never able to have." Marion's words were full of emotions I couldn't quite grasp.

This couldn't be real.

She reached forward and clasped my hand between both of hers. "Aria, you're family. You'll always be welcome here. Hopefully, by taking over Sanborn Place, you'll finally realize you're one of ours." Her hands were warm, her grasp frail yet firm.

I stared into her golden-brown eyes, my heart blooming inside my chest. Her eyes were so much like my own. A physical feature that connected me to the family I hadn't been born into, but that accepted me anyway.

Could she really mean it?

"This isn't right." Sanborn Place was Mike's life. He'd started the company from nothing. I'd been a merc for only a handful of years. I knew I hadn't earned my stripes. "I don't deserve it. You should keep it. Hell, you should sell it. I know the money could help you live comfortably. You deserve that."

Decision made, I implored her with my eyes. I couldn't keep something this important. No matter how badly I wanted to. I could find work at another guild. I had savings. I'd be fine. "Sell it. If it's in my name already, I'll sign it over to you. It's yours."

Marion gently touched my cheek, her eyes soft.

"It's yours. Sanborn Place took my husband from me. I want no part of it." Her tone broached no argument. "His client files are in this box." She indicated a large cardboard file box beside the sofa. "He kept copies of everything at home so you won't have to worry about those lost in the fire."

I flinched. I wanted to apologize for the fire. For taking away his body and leaving her nothing but ash to bury. But I couldn't. I didn't trust myself not to fall apart.

When Mike was killed, it was like someone ripped my heart from my chest. Nightmares plagued me. I lost my appetite. I could feel myself wasting away, but none of it mattered. Not when—

Marion's voice interrupted my thoughts. "I didn't want you facing it the way it was, so I hired a crew to repair the damage. They told me they should complete renovations within the next two weeks." Marion reached into the pocket of her sweater and retrieved a business card, handing it to me. "You're welcome to stop by the site anytime, and the owner assured me you can call anytime if you have questions or want to make any changes."

Diamond Rock Construction was written across the black surface in simple but sleek embossed lettering. I rubbed a finger over the smooth soft matte finish. The only other information on the card was a phone number, no personal name to go with it.

"Sanborn Place is yours. Don't feel like you can't make changes."

I stayed for another hour, doing my best to remain upbeat. Marion fixed the two of us lunch from the variety of casseroles friends and relatives had brought over. I pushed the food around my plate, hoping it looked like I was actually eating, but I was pretty sure Marion caught on when she continued to offer me alternatives. Pie. Rice Pudding. Kale salad. It all looked great, but my stomach revolted at the idea of being filled with any of it.

She'd barely touched her own food. The grief weighing on her was all too visible, as though it were a physical thing. I wished I knew what to say, how to help.

As I prepared to leave, I promised Marion I'd stay in touch and visit often. I wasn't sure if it was a promise I could keep. My guilt over Mike's death ate at me every minute of every day. Part of me thought it'd be easier if Marion decided she didn't want to see me again.

It was a selfish thought.

❧

Aria's story continues in
KISSED BY FIRE
Grab your copy now on Amazon

Heya!

Thank you so much for giving *Cursed by Fire* a read. When I first started writing this book, I'll be honest, I had no idea what I was doing. All I knew was that I had an idea and I really wanted to see it come to life. Cursed by Fire may not be perfect, lord knows Aria Naveed certainly isn't. She has a lot of growing to do but I hope you'll continue this little adventure with me because I'm excited to see where we end up.

If you're interested in continuing on this rollercoaster ride, I have good news and bad news.

The good news is that Kissed by Fire, book two in the Blood & Magic series is out now! The bad news, Aria is up against tough odds and a pesky Chupacabra is determined to have her for dinner.

Add in a rogue vampire and a bite with some life changing consequences and we have a recipe for disaster.

Just follow the link and Grab your Copy!

—> https://hi.switchy.io/KissedByFire

Xo Danielle

P.S. Reviews are like giving a hug to your favorite author. We love hugs. Please consider taking the time to leave a review for Cursed by Fire on Amazon!

P.S.S. Wanna chat? I love hearing from my readers, so if you're interested in staying connected, come visit me in my Facebook group at https://www.facebook.com/groups/danielleannett

Feedback: If you've found a problem with this ebook, let me know at DanielleAnnett@hotmail.com

Acknowledgments

There are so many people I want to thank for making this possible. First and foremost, ***Regina Wamba***. I entered your cover contest and happened to win and that sparked the moment I decided to take my writing seriously. Without that opportunity I don't know if I ever would have taken the plunge.

My husband who not once looked at me like I was a crazy person while I had imaginary conversations with my characters.

Jerica MacMillan who has become one of my very best and first author friends. You have no idea how much our friendship means to me.

Deb, for taking my rough book and helping me to polish it with shine.

To the blogger community. You guys are my everything. I never imaged the love and support I would receive and to say I am appreciative is an understatement.

*Thank you so very much, especially to **Cat** (Addicted 2 Heroines), **Traci** (Mad Hatter Reads), **Kimba** (Caffeinated Book Reviewer).*

And most of all, I'd like to thank you, my readers. Thank you for making my dreams come true. If it wasn't for you, I wouldn't have a reason to continue Aria's adventures. You make it happen by purchasing my books. Each and every one of you counts.

About the Author

Danielle Annett is a Latinx Author. She's snarky AF, has three rad minions, and likes to write about kick butt heroines in volatile settings. Born and raised in sunny California she now resides in the Pacific Northwest, home to her Pacific Northwest Pack.

Sign up and get notified when Danielle has a new release: https://hi.switchy.io/AnnettNews

Find out more about Danielle here:
Website: www.Danielle-Annett.com
Amazon: https://hi.switchy.io/1AeV
Reader Group: http://www.facebook.com/groups/danielleannett
Facebook: http://www.facebook.com/AuthorDanielleAnnett
Bookbub: https://hi.switchy.io/AnnettBB
Instagram: https://www.instagram.com/authordanielleannett/
Goodreads: https://www.goodreads.com/author/show/7771866.Danielle_Annett
Audible: https://hi.switchy.io/ANNETTAUDIBLE

Stay in Touch

And before you go
Please consider leaving an honest review.
Reviews are like giving your favorite author a hug and we really love ***hugs!***